Brian Sears is a trained teacher wi
primary education. He was head teac
Green, Hertfordshire from 1980 unti
now continues teaching in one-to-one private tuition.

In 1984, Brian had six stories published by NCEC in an anthology, A
Yearful of Stories, and has contributed to the SU Bible reading notes,
Snapshots, for primary school aged children. For the last nine football
seasons, Brian has realized his other passion, in that he has written a
weekly column in The Independent based around statistics of Premier-
ship football. Four years ago, Scripture Union and CPO jointly published
Brian's record of Christians working in the football industry, Goal!
Winning, Losing and Life, the writing of which involved Brian in
meeting the likes of Cyrille Regis, and a memorable visit to Old Trafford to
interview Manchester United's secretary and chaplain.

Brian frequently leads church services by invitation in Hertfordshire,
mainly in the Baptist tradition. He is an enthusiastic Watford FC
supporter, two highlights being the play-off victory four years ago at
Wembley and telling a story about another of his favourite characters,
Timothy Bear, at the club's annual carol service.

Brian's book, Through the Year with Timothy Bear, was published by
BRF in 2006.

Text copyright © Brian Sears 2007
The author asserts the moral right
to be identified as the author of this work

Published by
The Bible Reading Fellowship
First Floor, Elsfield Hall
15–17 Elsfield Way, Oxford OX2 8FG
Website: www.brf.org.uk

ISBN-10: 1 84101 393 5
ISBN-13: 978 1 84101 393 0
First published 2007
10 9 8 7 6 5 4 3 2 1 0

Acknowledgments
Unless otherwise stated, scripture quotations are taken from the Contemporary
English Version of the Bible published by HarperCollins Publishers, copyright ©
1991, 1992, 1995 American Bible Society.

Scripture quotations from THE MESSAGE. Copyright © by Eugene H. Peterson
1993, 1994, 1995. Used by permission of NavPress Publishing Group.

A catalogue record for this book is available from the British Library

Printed in Singapore by Craft Print International Ltd

Famous Prayers
Unpacked

—— 26 five-minute stories ——

exploring The Lord's Prayer and the
prayer of St Francis

Lord, make me an instrument of your peace.

Our Father in heaven

Brian Sears

Acknowledgments

Tom Wetherby and his family have evolved over many years. They began weekday life as the characters for assembly stories at Yorke Mead School in Croxley Green, where I taught for 23 years. On Sundays, the stories grew up in local churches including Rickmansworth Baptist Church, Kingswood Baptist Church, Watford, and my home church, Croxley Green Baptist. More recently, I have prepared them for publication at Little Green School in Croxley Green.

A colleague from my teaching days, Mrs Chris Luddington, has made many helpful suggestions. My wife, Ros, has been constantly supportive, not least in her keyboard skills, and Jennifer and Katherine, our daughters, have adopted the Wetherby family as their own.

The Lord's Prayer

Our Father in heaven,
hallowed be your name.
Your kingdom come,
your will be done,
on earth as in heaven
Give us today our daily bread.
Forgive us our sins,
as we forgive those who sin against us.
Lead us not into temptation,
but deliver us from evil.
For the kingdom, the power and the glory are yours.
Now and for ever. Amen

The prayer of St Francis

Lord, make me an instrument of your peace,
Where there is hatred, let me sow love;
where there is injury, pardon;
where there is doubt, faith;
where there is despair, hope;
where there is darkness, light;
where there is sadness, joy;

O Divine Master, grant that I may not so much seek
to be consoled as to console;
to be understood as to understand;
to be loved as to love.
For it is in giving that we receive;
it is in pardoning that we are pardoned;
and it is in dying that we are born to eternal life.

Contents

The prayer of St Francis

Introduction

In this book you will find 26 read-aloud stories based on the character of Tom Wetherby, a young boy who enjoys the kind of everyday adventures recognized by children everywhere. There are 13 stories to help explore the meaning of the Lord's Prayer and 13 to help explore the themes of the prayer for peace, widely attributed to St Francis of Assisi. Each of the stories links into a phrase from these famous prayers.

The Lord's Prayer

The Lord's Prayer is the model of prayer that Jesus taught to his disciples. In the Gospels it can be found in Matthew 6:9–13 and Luke 11:2–4. It is a great encouragement for a teacher when he or she is asked by a class or a group to teach them something special. How pleased Jesus must have been when his disciples said to him, 'Lord, teach us to pray.' Their request was the prompt for the prayer that is now prayed by thousands of people every day. Something of the meaning contained in this wonderful prayer is unpacked for children through Tom's adventures. The prayer is presented in modern language, but traditional language can be substituted if children are more familiar with that version.

The prayer of St Francis

St Francis was born in Assisi, Italy, in 1182, around the time that Robin Hood is thought to have been living in Sherwood Forest, England. After a carefree youth, Francis turned his back on his inherited wealth and committed himself to God. Like many early saints, he lived a very simple life of poverty and, in so doing, gained a reputation for being the friend of animals. He established the rule of St Francis, which exists today as the Order of St Francis, or the Franciscans. He died in 1226, aged 44. His prayer includes many of the biblical truths that uphold Christian values, so even if Francis did not pray this prayer line by line, he certainly practised it and it has come down to us as a pattern to follow.

Bible links and follow up

Each story is accompanied by an appropriate Bible link, suggesting which Bible passage or story might best be used in conjunction with the phrase of the prayer being explored. Follow-up material for the assembly or classroom includes ways to help children to:

★ get to grips with the story
★ express the story
★ own the story
★ live out the story

The stories can be used in collective worship and assemblies, PSHE and Circle Time, as an aid to the teaching of RE, or purely for enjoyment at story time.

The Lord's Prayer

Some grandad

 Bible link

When Jesus had finished praying, one of his disciples said to him, 'Lord, teach us to pray, just as John taught his followers to pray.' So Jesus told them, 'Pray in this way:

Our Father in heaven...

LUKE 11:1–2a AND MATTHEW 6:9a

As Tom Wetherby has grown older, he has found out more and more about his grandad. He has found out, for example, that Grandad Wetherby used to be in the Air Force. Grandma showed Tom the medals his grandad had been awarded.

'He flew planes for the RAF,' she told him. 'He was promoted to Group Captain,' she added proudly. Tom thought that sounded grand: Group Captain Wetherby.

'But I shall still call him Grandad,' said Tom.

Then it turned out that Grandad had been an athlete, a long-distance runner. He had won a 10,000 metres race for the county where they still lived. Grandma showed Tom more medals and some cups from when Grandad had been a lot younger.

Another thing was Grandad's work. He had been a manager and then managing director at a local firm. There had been a big article in the paper when the firm was awarded the Queen's award for exports. Tom had read all about it and taken the cutting to school. Now Grandad was retiring and he had been invited to a garden party with the Queen at Buckingham Palace. What a famous, important grandad!

It was typical of Grandad that on the day of the garden party he arranged to give Tom a treat as well.

'I can't take you with me to the palace for the tea party, but we'll go sightseeing first and then you can come home with your father when he finishes at the office.' Tom couldn't wait. A day in London with Grandad to himself!

When the day came, Grandad Wetherby was all dressed up in his best suit, fit for the Queen. He was full of information and stories about London. Tom listened, enjoying every moment. After dinner, grandad and grandson arrived at the Tower of London. A zigzag path took them down a steep slope towards a car park. It was then that Tom spoilt the day. He took it into his head to take a short cut, leaving the path and going straight down the steep, grassy slope, in spite of the warning signs.

'No, Tom!' shouted Grandad, but it was too late. The steepness of his chosen route made Tom's legs work faster and faster until they were out of control. Tom lost his footing and tumbled head over heels to crash on the grey tarmac. The last glimpse that Tom saw before unconsciousness swept over him was of Grandad, in spite of his best suit, leaping down the same slope that had been too much for Tom.

When Tom regained consciousness, the first thing he saw was that best suit of Grandad by the side of his hospital bed. Grandad squeezed his hand and winked.

'Shouldn't you be with the Queen?' murmured Tom.

'Never mind about that. It's much more important to get you right. There's quite a bump on your head, so I'll just sit here with you until your dad arrives from his office.'

Just before he went off to sleep again, Tom thought about that. Grandad thought it was more important to be with his grandson—his silly grandson who hadn't kept to the path— than to be at Buckingham Palace.

'That's my grandad all over,' thought Tom.

Helping children get to grips with the story

★ Even though God, our Father in heaven, is not mentioned in the story, which character has most to teach us about what God is like?

★ Which character has most to teach us about what we are like?

★ Did Tom find out about his grandad all at once? How did he build up his knowledge?

Ways for children to express the story

★ Write or tell a story called 'Not doing as I was told'.

★ Draw a picture of Tom tumbling down the slope.

Helping children to own the story

★ What mistakes did Tom make? Do we make those kind of mistakes?

★ How can we build up our picture of what God is like?

Ways for children to live out the story

★ Talk to someone you trust about their beliefs in God.
★ What are some of the things you already know about God?
★ Is God only in heaven? What do you think about heaven?

An important question

 Bible link

… help us to honour your name.
MATTHEW 6:9b

Tom Wetherby is sometimes full of questions.

'You and your curiosity,' says his mum.

It's often when Mrs Wetherby is tucking him in bed for the night that the questions come tumbling out. 'Questions and prayers', they call it.

Mother and son were just getting ready for prayers when Tom looked round his room and asked, 'Where is God?'

His mum found herself—as she often does—thinking very quickly.

'You keep a good lookout tomorrow, Tom,' she said. 'When you come home, we'll check it out to see if God was around.'

By the morning, Tom had forgotten all about his question and the search his mum had set him. He had to walk to school with his mum and his little sister Charlotte, as Scott's mum had phoned to say that Scott had the 'shivers'. Tom would miss him.

Just past Scott's house, there was a house with a climbing plant all over its wall. It could have been a setting for *Jack and the Beanstalk*! On this sunny October morning, the plant was ablaze with colour: yellows, oranges, golds, browns and purples. Tom just stood there spellbound. The plant was beautiful! It was unusual for Tom to be so still so long; normally he would have been chattering to Scott.

At school, Tom's teacher Mrs Evans was her bright and cheerful self. Her class settled happily and then it was time for assembly. It was going to be the usual assembly, with their head teacher, Mr Watson, telling a story. Tom found the story especially gripping. It was about a young man called Joseph being given a multi-coloured coat with long sleeves for his birthday. Joseph then fell out with his ten older brothers by dreaming that he would boss them about. They got their own back by throwing Joseph down a dry well in the desert.

Mr Watson told the story in exciting detail. Tom could picture it all. It left him looking forward to the next episode. The story stayed with Tom as they all sang a song from a musical about Joseph's multi-coloured coat.

Tom had other things to think about in maths. He liked practical maths lessons, using instruments and making shapes. Last term, Tom had discovered how good he was with compasses. 'You've got a real talent there,' praised Mrs Evans.

Today the class were to make flower patterns using compasses. Then they could colour them in. Tom's was a super pattern; everything fitted exactly. The six petals just appeared. Tom did his work very carefully and the finished product met with Mrs Evans' enthusiastic approval.

'It was easy really. The compasses did the work for me,' said Tom modestly.

Things did not go so well at dinner time. Even though it was autumn, the children could still play cricket on the field, as the weather was so good. Cricket is Tom's favourite summer game. It was his turn to bat, and then Spencer's. For once, Tom was having a good, long innings, but it came to a painful conclusion. As he was running hard to make a second run, the ball that was flung towards the stumps hit Tom, by accident, on the side of his leg.

Ow! His hand felt the spot. There was no blood, but a swelling in the shape of an egg was growing out of his skin and it certainly hurt. Spencer had his arm round him.

'I'll take you inside,' Spencer said calmly.

'But it's your turn to bat,' objected Tom.

'This is much more important,' continued Spencer, 'especially with your best friend Scott away.'

Spencer was as good as his word. He stayed with Tom while Mrs Sullivan, their school nurse, felt the side of Tom's leg.

'There's not too much damage, but we'll see if your mum is at home. Home's the best place for you with a bad leg,' said the kindly Mrs Sullivan.

Mrs Wetherby was at home and Tom was soon back there with her. It was a surprise to be spending the afternoon so quietly.

'I suppose it was hard to find where God was today,' said Mrs Wetherby after a while.

'Oh dear,' said Tom, 'I forgot to look.'

'Can't you remember anything that happened?' asked his mum.

Then Tom remembered the beautiful plant, the story about Joseph, the exact pattern of the flower in maths and Spencer being willing to give up his innings.

'It wouldn't surprise me,' said his mum, 'if God was in all those things and a lot more. And if it wasn't for that bump on the leg, we wouldn't be sitting here discovering how much God is into.'

'Amazing!' exclaimed Tom, feeling the lump on his leg. 'Do you think one day I'll play cricket for England?'

'You and your questions,' laughed Mrs Wetherby.

Helping children get to grips with the story

★ Why did Tom notice more things than usual on the way to school? What did he notice and what might you notice?
★ How did Spencer show that he is a good friend?
★ What was good about a nasty bump on Tom's leg?

Ways for children to express the story

★ Draw a colourful plant.
★ Find the story Tom heard in assembly, in the Bible. You will find it in Genesis 37:2–24.
★ Draw a pattern of shapes—maybe the flower pattern in the story, using compasses.

Helping children to own the story

★ To 'hallow' God's name is to keep it special. How can we do that with regard to what God has made and the way he arranges things?
★ Which things around you do you find beautiful to look at, and how can we help to keep them like that?
★ When things have gone wrong—like being hit by a ball—can you think of any good things that have come out of them?

Ways for children to live out the story

★ How would you answer the question, 'Where is God?'
★ How can God's name be kept special?
★ How can God's name be spoilt?

To buy well, shop with Nell!

Bible link

Come and set up your kingdom…
MATTHEW 6:10a

Tom's class were to visit the local market. Mrs Evans told them that they were going to become reporters, producing a special edition of *Market Mail*.

'I'm fed up with all the bad news we keep reading in our papers,' she said. 'So I want you to include some good news stories wherever you can.' The class buzzed with excitement.

On arrival at the market, the class were given last-minute reminders about the task in hand and arrangements that would keep them safe. Tom was given the area around a stall called 'Nell's grocery'. He looked and listened very carefully, occasionally jotting down words and observations on his clipboard.

The lady in front of the stall—she must be Nell—was a large woman with red cheeks on a face that often smiled. Her clothes were old and patched, but she looked very clean. Her hands were spotless as she put food into paper bags. When she took the money, she slipped on a pair of gloves to handle it.

As Tom watched, an old woman came up, leaning heavily on her walking stick.

'Three eggs, please,' she said to Nell.

Nell smiled, and keen-eyed Tom saw her push four eggs gently into the bag and still only charge the old woman for three.

Other people went by and bought nothing from Nell's stall. In fact, Tom overheard one woman say, 'I wouldn't go to that stall for all the tea in China. That stall belongs to Smelly Nelly.' She went on her way, laughing unkindly.

A man came to Nell's stall to buy groceries. With him were two unhappy children, crying and squabbling.

'Their mum is in hospital and I don't know what to do with them,' explained the man to Nell.

'These will keep them quieter,' said Nell, and handed a lollipop to each child. 'And there's no charge,' added Nell, spotting the man's hand going to his pocket. The crying stopped as the licking began.

Tom had hardly written all this down when there was shouting and excitement all round him. A chase was taking place among the market stalls. The owner of the jewellery stall was pursuing a man in a bobble hat, shouting, 'Thief! Thief!'

As the accused man sprinted past Tom, a flash of silver escaped from his pocket and rolled under the corner of Nell's stall. The man from the jewellery stall came to a stop between Tom and Nell's stall.

'It was my most valuable silver ring,' he gasped. His head flopped down and his eyes spotted the ring.

'Smelly Nelly,' he blurted out. 'You've got it! He was passing it on to you. You're in with the thief. Smelly Nelly's a crook!'

Poor Nell. No one had ever called her Smelly Nelly to her face before. Tears stung her eyes. Tom knew he could not remain behind his clipboard. Sometimes reporters need to make the news. He stepped forward.

'I saw what happened. The man in the bobble hat dropped the ring by accident. It just happened to roll there. I've been watching Nell anyway.'

Tom consulted his notes and reported about Nell's cleanliness, her free egg to an elderly customer and the lollipops for squabbling children.

'And I'll tell you the headline of my report: "To buy well, shop with Nell."'

Quite a crowd had gathered and Tom realized he'd given a sort of speech. The jewellery man knew he'd been too quick to judge.

Back in class, Mrs Evans gave a prize for the best report in *Market Mail*. The prize was a packet of the most delicious chocolate biscuits. Mrs Evans awarded it to Tom.

'It won't surprise you,' she said, 'that I bought them from a stall in the market belonging to Nell. As I queued up, I heard several customers congratulating themselves. They said, "To buy well, shop with Nell!"'

Helping children get to grips with the story

★ What did Mrs Evans mean by 'good news' and 'bad news'?
★ What did different people think about Nell?
★ How did Tom the news reporter turn into Tom the news maker?

Ways for children to express the story

★ Write a poem about a market or shopping centre.
★ Draw a portrait of Nell.
★ Write your own 'good news' story as if it was going into a newspaper.

Helping children to own the story

★ What sort of things do you think God wants to have in his kingdom?
★ In what ways was the market *not* like God's kingdom?
★ In what ways did the market become more like that kingdom?

Ways for children to live out the story

★ Have you ever had the wrong impression of what a person is really like? What changed your mind about them?
★ The market became more like God's kingdom. Where else can that happen? What needs to be done to make it happen?

Your will be done on earth as it is in heaven

Don't DIY

 Bible link

... so that everyone on earth will obey you, as you are obeyed in heaven.
MATTHEW 6:10b

Tom's mum had been on about it for months—her bedroom!

'It's all bits and pieces,' she said. 'I haven't got enough hanging space. I'm ashamed to show it to anyone.'

Tom's dad stalled for time. He didn't need so much hanging space. Who was there to show it to anyway? The two children, Tom and Charlotte, felt like referees.

Mrs Wetherby brought matters to a head when she waved her *Dreamland* catalogue at her husband and said that it would only cost £4,000 to get a new bedroom fitted professionally.

'All right,' muttered Mr Wetherby, 'we'll visit the do-it-yourself showrooms on Saturday.'

The whole family went. It was a kind of outing. What a place! There was every item of furniture, in such a variety of styles and colours. The bedroom suite going at half its usual price looked lovely, and Tom's mum smiled winningly.

'All right. We'll have it,' decided Dad.

Tom and Charlotte were surprised when the furniture all came in flat boxes to be carried away. Their dad looked worried.

'It's no trouble to put together, sir,' said the polite young salesman. 'Anyone with any sense and a screwdriver can put it together in a couple of hours.'

Tom smiled encouragingly at his dad, although he knew that the shelves Mr Wetherby had built in Tom's room sloped quite alarmingly in places.

'That should be straightforward, then,' said Mr Wetherby.

'You can't go wrong, sir, and you'll find the instructions so helpful.'

What fun it was, unpacking the boxes at home. It seemed like a gigantic jigsaw puzzle. Tom was given the job of ticking off the list of parts. His dad smiled nervously.

'You're just as good as me at Lego,' said Tom helpfully.

Three hours later, even the nervous smile had disappeared and it was time for the gritting of teeth. Tom's mum was inside half a wardrobe, trying to join it up to the other half.

His dad was shouting, 'Push a bit harder… dear!'

There was a cracking sound. 'Not too hard… dear!'

'We must be missing something!'

Tom finally came to the rescue.

'You know the new family next door? Well, Alex says his dad is quite handy. Shall I go and see if he's free?'

'Certainly not! It must be quite straightforward. Where are the instructions?'

'But Alex says his dad has quite a bit of common sense,' continued Tom, receiving a withering look from Mr Wetherby.

An hour later, Tom's dad gave in. Tom was detailed to go next door. His mum stepped out of half a wardrobe, tripped over the ledge and the side fell on to the carpet.

'We'll see what clever clogs can do,' said Mr Wetherby through gritted teeth.

Alex's dad smiled broadly when he entered the bedroom.

'You don't happen to know my job, do you?' he asked. 'It's designing furniture for do-it-yourself shops! And I know this particular system well.'

Thirty minutes later, Alex's dad and Tom's dad surveyed the finished work. It looked just as it had in the showroom. Tom's mum linked her arm through her husband's.

'It looks really great... dear,' she said.

'A marvellous design and a marvellous designer,' said Mr Wetherby. 'It's much better knowing the one who made the furniture and putting it together with him.'

Helping children get to grips with the story

★ How did Tom's mum feel about the ways the bedroom needed changing? How did his dad feel about it?
★ In what different ways could Tom's dad be helped to put the new bedroom together?
★ God is putting a whole world together. How does he let us know how we can help him do it?

Ways for children to express the story

★ Share experiences of do-it-yourself successes and disasters in your family.
★ Design and make a model piece of furniture out of card.

Helping children to own the story

★ What's the best or the most difficult thing you've ever made? Which things or people helped you?
★ Think of people you know who are especially good at something. Think and talk about what you might learn from them.

Ways for children to live out the story

★ How good are you at asking for help to do things?
★ How good are you at giving help to do things?
★ What does God give us to help us make earth more like heaven?
★ Think of some things that God wants for our world. How can you help them to come about?

Give us today our daily bread

Cheese sandwiches!

 Bible link

Give us our food for today.
MATTHEW 6:11

Tom's grandad and grandma were going on holiday.

'We'll have a treat before we go,' Grandad said to Tom. 'We'll have a special meal.'

'Great,' replied Tom. Their last special meal had been at a fast-food restaurant in the high street that Tom particularly enjoys. Doubtless it would be the same again.

It was arranged that the day before Grandad's and Grandma's holiday Tom would spend the whole day with them. It all started off so well, with cricket on the lawn. They made up a new rule that it would count as six runs if you hit Grandma's washing basket. Tom was getting into quite a long innings when Grandma called Grandad to answer the phone.

'There's a problem with our friend's car,' he reported when he returned. 'He wants my help. It shouldn't take long and I'll be back. Grandma will look after you.'

Tom turned away, disappointed. Grandma was all right, but not so much fun as Grandad—more boring, somehow.

'I can bowl underarm,' said Grandma, smiling, as Grandad closed the gate behind him. Tom went to drive Grandma's first bowl down towards the workshed, but the ball kept low and thudded into his wicket. Out! Bowled out by Grandma's first ball! Tom was furious. He flung the bat down and stamped off towards Grandad's workshed.

'You mustn't go in there on your own,' reminded Grandma. 'There are too many sharp tools around. Go indoors and play with the train set.'

'Very well,' said Tom grumpily, 'but it's all so boring.'

Tom sat in the spare bedroom, chin on his hands, doing little except longing for Grandad and his special treat. At last he heard footsteps coming up the stairs, but it was only Grandma.

'Dinner time, Tom,' she announced.

'I don't feel hungry,' lied Tom. 'I'm waiting for Grandad.'

'Come on, Tom,' persisted Grandma. 'We can't be sure how long Grandad will be. It's your favourite, too: chicken and chips followed by treacle tart and ice cream.'

'No, thank you,' muttered Tom through clenched teeth. 'I'm not eating anything.'

Not even his favourite meal could change Tom's mood. Grandma's smile was gone and her shoulders drooped. She went sadly back downstairs.

Half an hour later, Tom heard someone upstairs again. This time it was Grandad, drying his hands on a towel. His face was stern and, for once, his steel-blue eyes had lost their sparkle. Tom failed to notice the warning signs.

'Get your things together, Tom, and come with me in the car.'

'Great,' thought Tom to himself, 'we'll be off to the high street.'

The journey was not, however, to the high street, but back to Tom's home. Grandad turned off the engine and opened the door for Tom.

'See you after our holiday,' said Grandad in a soft voice.

'But,' blurted out Tom, 'what about my treat at the restaurant?'

'Grandma's meal was the special treat. She was up at seven o'clock this morning making sure everything would be ready. Off you go, Tom.'

Tom's mum was already at the front gate. Her face showed that she already knew what had happened. Grandad drove off. Tom stood on the pavement miserably. It had all gone so wrong.

'Straight to your room, young man,' she said, pointing up the stairs.

Tom had a long time to think things through, getting hungrier by the minute. When he flicked on his television, there was even more food for thought. A programme was only too clearly showing the hunger of children in an African country plagued by drought and disruption.

Tom remembered Grandma's meal that he had so recently turned down. What an idiot he had been! At last he was sorting himself out. He would begin to put things right.

The first step was to remember to say 'thank you' for the cheese sandwiches that Mum brought up for him later that afternoon.

Helping children get to grips with the story

★ What made Tom feel cheerful in the story?
★ What made Tom feel miserable in the story?
★ At the end of the story, Tom took the first step to put things right. What was that first step? What other steps could he take?

Ways for children to express the story

★ Make a list of your favourite foods. Finish off the list with a food you don't really enjoy at all and write 'ugh' after it.
★ See if you can find out about somewhere in the world where there is not enough food, or not enough variety of foods.

Helping children to own the story

★ Are there some foods that you know are good for you, but you don't enjoy eating? What do you do when you are given those foods?
★ Did Tom deserve his punishment? Was it a suitable punishment?

Ways for children to live out the story

★ What do you think is meant in the Lord's Prayer by 'daily bread'?
★ Why did Jesus say we should pray for *our* daily bread and not *my* daily bread?
★ Who should we thank for our food? Do we do it?

Don't touch the trifle

 Bible link

Forgive us for doing wrong…
MATTHEW 6:12a

Tom always feels a bit left out around Charlotte's birthday time. His mum and dad do their best to be fair, but naturally Charlotte takes centre stage for her birthday. This year, the day before that special occasion, Mum arranged to take her daughter out to buy a new party dress.

'We won't be long. Make sure you don't touch the trifle!' she said.

Tom had watched his mum make the special trifle. It had fruit at the bottom with sponge mixed in, jelly in the middle, and just now she had poured the pink blancmange on top. She'd put it in the fridge for the next day's party.

Halfway through the morning, Tom was thirsty. He came down from his bedroom into the kitchen and poured himself a fizzy drink. It was easy to check that everything was all right in the fridge. Yes! There was the trifle on the topmost shelf.

'Don't touch the trifle!' echoed his mum's voice inside his head.

Tom went back up to his bedroom and printed out the picture he had drawn on his computer. His dad was down at the bottom of the garden, digging over the vegetable patch, so there was no one to show it to. Tom began to miss his sister and, with nothing else to do, he decided he was hungry.

He returned to the kitchen, but the biscuit tin was empty. He opened the fridge door. Certainly that trifle looked appetizing! It was worth a closer look. Mum had told him not to touch the trifle, but she hadn't said anything about the bowl. He could appreciate it more fully at table level.

His hands circled the bowl and gently lifted it off the shelf. Carefully, he brought the trifle safely to the kitchen table. Tom noticed that the blancmange was a long way from setting. It flowed from side to side.

Tom had an idea. He fetched a spoon from the drawer and removed a spoonful of pink blancmange. The rest of the blancmange covered over perfectly. No one would know it was missing. And it tasted delicious!

If it worked once, it would work many times—but Tom hadn't realized the extent of his hunger. Squelch! Tom's spoon finally dug into the jelly, which certainly was set. There was no hiding that jagged hole.

Miserably, Tom returned to his bedroom to await the inevitable. Soon he heard the key in the front door, an excited sister entering... and then his mum's voice.

'Tom! Come here at once!'

Tom was sent back to his bedroom. Even though it was

only two o'clock in the afternoon, he had to get right into bed.

Tom was on his own a long time, and it was his mum and dad together who next came into his room. The wrongdoing of the afternoon was fully explored and parental disappointment fully expressed. When there was a pause, Tom said, 'I'm truly sorry. If I could have this afternoon over again, it would be totally different.'

'How do we know that you're really sorry?' demanded his dad. But then he did know, as a tear fell from his son's eye and exploded on the duvet.

'All right,' said his mum. 'I'll let you make a new trifle with me early tomorrow morning.'

When it came to Charlotte's party, Tom knew he'd been truly forgiven. He was even allowed a second helping of the special trifle with fruit and sponge at the bottom, jelly in the middle and delicious pink blancmange on top of that!

Helping children get to grips with the story

★ There's one main thing that Tom did in the story that was wrong. What was it, and can you spot any others?
★ How did Tom feel after he had eaten the blancmange and before his mum came home? Would it have been all right just to have taken one spoonful?
★ How do we know that Tom was truly sorry and that he was truly forgiven? Look for several reasons.

Ways for children to express the story

★ Write down Tom's thoughts after he had been sent to bed.
★ Draw or make a collage of the trifle.

Helping children to own the story

★ Think of other examples of disobedience. An early one in the Bible might come to mind. Talk about them.
★ How does it feel to be truly forgiven?

Ways for children to live out the story

★ Who needed to forgive Tom? Don't forget in your thinking that the story is illustrating part of a prayer. When we do things that are wrong, who needs to forgive us?
★ Disobedience is the wrong thing in this story that needs forgiveness. What other wrong things could stories be made up about, that would need forgiving?

As we forgive those who sin against us

A brace for Charlotte

Bible link
… as we forgive others.
MATTHEW 6:12b

Tom's sister, Charlotte, had to go to the dentist. She didn't have toothache but her teeth were growing crooked.

'Your mouth is far too crowded,' reported the dentist. 'I'll have to take one or two out and then it will be best for you to wear a brace for a while.'

When it was time to wear the brace, Charlotte found it most uncomfortable. It was a contraption of wire and plastic that seemed much too big for her mouth. If Charlotte's mouth was too crowded before the brace came, it seemed much worse now.

'Short-term pain brings long-term gain!' announced Dad, pleased with his burst of wisdom. Charlotte wondered if her dad had ever had to wear a brace himself, but she was having too much difficulty speaking clearly to say anything. Eating was hard, too. When she swallowed, it was all too easy to dribble.

'You don't have to wear it at night, Charlotte, but you do have to wear it all day at home and at school,' said Mum, looking up from the dentist's letter.

Wearing the brace at school was a great trial for Charlotte. It felt so awkward. She couldn't hide it. Everyone knew she was different even when her mouth was closed. It sorted out who her true friends were, especially at play time. Some children made faces at her, pretending they too had a brace round their teeth. Then they talked as if their mouths were full. Charlotte swallowed hard… and dribbled.

'Baby, baby Charlotte,' called a voice.

'Braces to hold your trousers up,' said Scott, feeling clever.

But worst of all was when even Tom joined in. 'Brace, brace for funny face,' yelled out her brother.

How could he? Children on the playground laughed out loud. Charlotte wasn't laughing. She only just managed not to cry. It was all right for them; it was all right for Tom. They had the right number of teeth. They didn't need to wear a contraption to make their teeth grow straight.

The next week, it was Tom's turn to be in the wars. He tripped over in the playground, fell headlong and grazed his nose on the tarmac. It didn't bleed much but it needed dabbing. He was sent in to see Mrs Sullivan, the school nurse.

'Well, I can't very well bandage up your nose, Tom. We'll have to let the air get to it.'

Tom went back on the playground. He was upset. His nose did hurt. Then someone called out, 'Look! Here comes Rudolph!'

Tom glared round to find out who it was.

'Nose, nose like a blooming rose,' said clever Scott.

Charlotte saw Tom's anger. His hands were clenched and his eyebrows arched. She leapt between the older children. In spite of her brace, she had learnt to speak quite clearly again by now.

'Wait a minute!' she shouted slowly. 'How dare you be so nasty? How would you like to fall over and bleed?'

Everyone went quiet. A younger child had put them in their place. It was a lesson they would remember.

That night, at bedtime, Tom's mum found him near to tears.

'Is that nose of yours hurting?' she asked gently.

'No, it's not that,' managed Tom. 'It doesn't hurt much now.'

'Were they unkind to you?' wondered his mum.

'Some of them were, but I'm not upset about that.'

'What's the matter, then?' she asked.

Tom gave a sigh.

'Last week, I was so nasty to Charlotte about her brace, and today she was so nice to me about my nose.'

'Well,' said his mum, 'we learn things every day... even from sisters.'

She gave Tom a big wink. He tried to wink back but it made his nose ache too much. So he gave his mum a thumbs-up instead.

Helping children get to grips with the story

★ What made playtime difficult for Charlotte? How did playtime sort out who were Charlotte's real friends?
★ Why was Tom upset when his mum was seeing him to bed?

Ways for children to express the story

★ Draw a portrait of yourself looking different from normal in some way.
★ Talk about a time in your life when you've been hurt, either on your body or inside yourself.

Helping children to own the story

★ Think of times when you have been forgiven or have forgiven someone else. What do you remember?
★ Charlotte could have reacted very differently from the way she did when Tom came back to the playground. What could she have done? What do we call that kind of behaviour? (Getting your own back, or retaliation.)

Ways for children to live out the story

★ Suggest some good rules for playtimes.
★ Do being sorry and being forgiven always need words?
★ Do adults still need to be forgiving and forgiven?

Lead us not into temptation

A collection to be proud of

Bible link

Keep us from being tempted…
MATTHEW 6:13a

....

Tom adds to his collection of model planes as often as he can. He buys kits that he puts together. He also has them as Christmas and birthday presents. He has become skilled at making the planes, and when they are finished, he hangs them from his bedroom ceiling. They're quite a sight. He takes visitors on conducted tours and always gains their admiration.

Grandad, having been Group Captain Wetherby, is particularly interested in Tom's collection.

'No Hurricane yet,' said Grandad, last time he was up in Tom's bedroom.

The Hurricane is Grandad's favourite plane.

'That's one of the most expensive model kits,' said Tom. 'It says £20.95 on the label in the shop. I'll have to wait until Christmas.'

There's a boy at Tom's school called Ashley, and he too is a collector of model planes. Last week he had news for Tom.

'That Hurricane model is a radical-looking plane when it's made up.'

'How on earth could you afford it?' asked Tom enviously.

'I got it from the model shop for nothing,' boasted Ashley.

It turned out that Ashley had gone to the shop for a tube of glue. When he paid for the glue, the shop assistant had put it in a very large bag as a sign that Ashley had paid for it. Ashley had stayed in the shop and, when nobody was looking, he'd slid the Hurricane model kit into the same bag. He left the shop unchallenged.

'But that's stealing,' gasped Tom.

'It was as easy as taking a rattle from a baby,' said an unconcerned Ashley.

It was strange, but by the end of school Tom had convinced himself that he needed some more glue, even though he had quite a full tube at home and no models left to assemble. He decided he would go to the model shop on his way home from school.

'Don't go. It's wrong!' a little voice seemed to say inside Tom.

He was only going for the glue. There was nothing wrong in that.

The model shop was not on his direct route home and Tom was almost surprised to find himself outside it, looking in wonder at the magnificent array of models in the window.

'Don't go inside. It's wrong!' insisted the voice again.

There was nothing wrong with buying a tube of glue, so he went inside the shop. He found his usual small tube of glue, took it to the counter, paid the 95p and it was his. Sure enough, the tube was placed in a bag that was much larger than necessary.

'It's the only size of bags that they make for us now,' commented the assistant. Tom turned away from the counter.

'Go straight home now,' whispered the voice inside him. 'There's no harm in looking round the shop,' said another part of Tom. He wandered round, getting nearer and nearer to the shelf where he knew he would find the Hurricane. At last he stood in front of it. Tom gauged the size of the box and the size of the bag. He was sure the box would slide into the bag. It was all too easy.

'Don't do it,' said the persistent little voice.

'It's far too expensive,' said a much bigger voice. Tom spun round.

'Grandad!'

'You'll have to wait for Christmas. I've a good idea you'll get one then,' smiled his grandad.

'Oh yes,' replied Tom. 'I was only looking. I came in for this glue.'

'What a big bag for a little tube of glue!' said Grandad in amazement.

'I thought that, too,' said Tom as grandad and grandson walked out of the shop.

'I'll see you home. I've got something to ask your mother.'

Back indoors, Grandad once again admired Tom's collection of model planes.

'You should be very proud of all this,' said Grandad, taking in the whole room at a glance. Tom nodded. He was glad that he still could be.

Helping children get to grips with the story

★ What were the stages of Tom's temptation?
★ In the story, a voice spoke inside Tom's head. What do we mean by that voice? Sometimes names are given to it. (Our conscience, our sense of right and wrong, or our principles.)
★ Why could Tom still be proud of his model aeroplane collection at the end of the story?

Ways for children to express the story

★ Draw pictures of a favourite hobby.
★ Write a script of different voices speaking inside Tom's head. Finish it off with Grandad's voice.

Helping children to own the story

★ Tom was tempted inside a shop. Where else might we be tempted and what things might we be tempted to do?
★ Why is it wrong to steal?

Ways for children to live out the story

★ Ashley appeared to have got away with stealing. It was so easy. How easy is it to do wrong things?
★ What things can we do so that we do not give in to temptation?

Pip to the rescue

 Bible link

… and protect us from evil.
MATTHEW 6:13b

....

When Grandma and Grandad go away on holiday, their dog, Pip, sometimes comes to stay with Tom and his family. Tom, especially, looks forward to such times. Pip is a lively Yorkshire terrier with trusting eyes and pointy ears. He's a great player of games like tug o' war and he's very obedient. Some say he takes after his master, Tom's grandad, and Tom's mum says, 'That dog is as good as gold.'

Last time Pip came to stay was at the time of Scott Stevens' birthday. He was going to have a party to celebrate and, of course, Tom was invited. It was to be tea followed by a video. Tom took Pip for a hurried walk round the block when he arrived home from school so that he wouldn't be late for the party.

Scott's mum had done splendidly with the food: lots of crisps with the sandwiches, lashings of cream with the trifle and cakes galore. With some relief, she sat the guests in front of the television for the video and retreated to her kitchen to clear up.

Unfortunately, Scott's mum hadn't been as careful with the choice of video as she had been with the food. She hadn't seen it and she didn't know anything about it, but the title should have been a warning: *Monster of Evil*.

Monster of Evil was a really nasty film. The boys watched in horror, but dared not say anything to each other. There were terrifying sequences of a monster. Everything and everyone he touched became mini-monsters of evil. It was a film of hatred, blackness and violence, with no hint of a happy ending.

As the credits rolled there was total silence among the boys. They were glad to get away to their homes. It hadn't turned out to be the kind of party that Scott had looked forward to so much.

The film stayed on Tom's mind all the way home, and it kept popping up again and again all evening. It was still with him when he was getting to sleep, so it was no surprise when it filled his dreams. He had to keep on escaping from the monster of evil. Once it was from a garden, next from a castle and then from a railway station.

Finally, he was in a garden shed that had the tiniest of windows. It was hot and dark and musty. The door swung closed with a click behind him and he knew that the monster was shut inside with him. There was no escape. He could not avoid being touched by the monster. He, too, would become hideous and evil. He screamed out.

'Help! Help! Help!'

To Tom's relief, there was not just him and the monster shut up in the shed. There was a wriggle of brown and a flash of trusting eyes. Pip was standing in the corner and barking for all he was worth.

To Tom's amazement, the monster froze in its tracks, then it began to tremble in a most unmonster-like way and started to shrink. When the monster was small enough, Pip pounced on it as if it had been a bone. Pip shook it and, wagging his tail, bounded to the dustbin. Tom lifted the lid and Pip disposed of the monster.

Tom's joy knew no bounds. The monster was no more. 'Good dog, good Pip!' he said, hugging the faithful animal in his arms.

Tom woke up. His hands were outside his bed and he really was stroking and hugging Pip. There beside Tom's bed, where he had never been allowed before, was Pip in real life. Pip was not even allowed upstairs!

'Come on, Pip. Let's get you back to your basket. Don't make a sound or we'll both be in trouble.'

Tom carried Pip silently downstairs to the kitchen. Pip rolled over and was almost immediately asleep. When Tom was back in bed, he was asleep just as quickly. But now it was Pip that filled his thoughts and his dreams. There was no longer any room for the monster of evil.

Helping children get to grips with the story

★ Why did Scott's party end in disappointment all round?
★ How did real life tie in with Tom's nightmare when he woke up?

Ways for children to express the story

★ Make a portrait of a pet (real or imagined) in words and pictures.
★ Draw an episode from Tom's nightmare.
★ Paint a picture of a monster.

Helping children to own the story

★ Have you watched something that has frightened you? How has it affected you? How do you cope with it?
★ Have you known what it is like to be comforted by a pet or a cuddly toy? Talk about it.

Ways for children to live out the story

★ As well as in films, in what other ways may we suddenly meet up with evil things in our lives?
★ How does God deliver us (protect us) from evil things?

For the kingdom is yours

The Royal Box

 Bible link

God made peace with you, and now he lets you stand in his presence as people who are holy and faultless and innocent.
COLOSSIANS 1:22b

The Wetherby family had been looking forward to Boxing Day for a long time. A special outing was in prospect.

Tom's dad had been friends with a boy called Max in his schooldays, and now he was called Uncle Max by the family. Uncle Max had become part-owner of a London theatre and he'd sent the Wetherby family tickets to join him on Boxing Day for the first performance of this year's pantomime. They weren't just any old tickets, but tickets for what the theatre calls its Royal Box. Sometimes members of the Queen's own family sat there. It was in the audience's view and oh, so comfortable.

Their theatre trip would be the climax of the Christmas arrangements for the Wetherbys—the icing on their Christmas cake, as it were.

Christmas, however, worked out badly for Tom. The holiday

started off with a far-from-good school report. Tom protested that life hadn't been easy since the hamster died, he'd been moved in class to sit between two girls, and his hand seemed to ache every time he took up a pen or pencil. Tom's mum and dad were not pleased and found his list of excuses unconvincing. It made Tom unusually moody.

In the end, Tom was surprised to get the mountain bike he had set his heart on as his main Christmas present. It had a horn that made it sound like a motorbike. As soon as breakfast was over, Tom was keen to show it off in the local park.

'But no trick riding, Tom,' warned his dad. 'Just get used to riding it.'

Tom's friends admired his new present.

'Just right for tricks,' said Scott. 'Follow me.'

Scott had had his bike last Christmas and it was a much more basic model. Surely, Tom would manage the stunts more easily on his. As he aimed his bike to leap over a log, Tom realized his mistake. The front wheel twisted round too easily and he crashed on landing.

Tom was unhurt but the mudguard was loose, the horn refused to work, and as he wheeled the bike home there was a regular clanking noise. Tom was furious with himself. Angrily, he kicked a stone in his path and then heard the sound of splintering glass as the stone landed in Mr Parker's garden.

Tom put his head down. Perhaps he hadn't been seen. He pushed the bike into the garage. It was Christmas dinner time.

It was the longest Christmas Day that Tom could ever

remember. He couldn't settle to anything. In his head, he kept hearing clanking noises mingling with the sounds of broken glass.

Tom went to bed without any protest, but not to sleep. He tossed and turned. How could he sit in a Royal Box with the Wetherby family? He recalled the events of the holiday. He was lazy, disobedient and cowardly. His mum and dad might deserve to be in the Royal Box—Charlotte as well—but certainly not him.

Tom decided he'd better run away. The rest of the family were in bed by now, getting the sleep they needed for the big day tomorrow. Tom dressed quickly and made his way silently to the top of the stairs. Then he froze.

'Where are you off to, my boy? I knew you weren't asleep. What's the matter?'

Tom clung to his dad and poured out the whole story. His father's face was stern, but his voice was kindly. A bike could be mended; the broken glass could be confessed. And Tom's dad had had one or two dodgy school reports in his time!

'You're a Wetherby. You certainly may sit in the Royal Box. None of us deserve such a treat; none of us could afford the tickets; Uncle Max has been so kind to all of us.'

So Tom did sit in the Royal Box. What an experience! What a family to belong to! His dad had begun that morning to repair the mountain bike. Tom had been round to see the Parkers. And as Tom finished the ice cream tub that Uncle Max brought him in the interval, he promised himself that next term's school report would be much improved!

Helping children get to grips with the story

★ What went wrong with Tom's Christmas? Why do you think it went wrong?
★ How did Mr Wetherby change Tom's mind about going to the theatre?

Ways for children to express the story

★ What do you think of the reasons Tom gave for his poor school report?
★ What would be your top three visits if they were given to you as a treat?

Helping children to own the story

★ When Jesus told stories about God's kingdom, he sometimes likened it to a tasty meal or a party. Jesus also told stories about forgiveness. One that is well known is often called the parable of the prodigal son. It's in Luke 15:11–32. How is it like this story about Tom?

Ways for children to live out the story

★ Have you ever spoilt something that has been given to you or done for you? Talk it over with some friends.
★ Do you prefer getting things by earning them or getting things as surprises?

The power is yours

The wall

 Bible link

The Lord helped Joshua in everything he did…
JOSHUA 6:27a

On Sunday, in church, the story had been about Joshua, the Israelites and the wall around Jericho. The story had been told in a most exciting way and Tom had felt involved in every part of it. He had almost run forward himself to help rescue Rahab and her family when the trumpets blew, the shout went up and the wall came down. What a mighty God, who could bring about such a victory!

On Monday, Tom was on half-term, so he went out in the garden with his special football. He'd won it in a competition and it had been signed by the local football team.

Tom started practising at the end of his garden, against a wall twice as tall as himself, which was built by the man living on the other side of it. He thought about what his mum and dad had said the other day about that neighbour.

'He keeps himself to himself,' said Dad.

'Yes,' agreed Mum. 'Anything to block out the world. Mind you, it's hard for him since his wife died.'

To Tom, the lonely neighbour was a mysterious, miserly man, but his wall was ideal for improving football skills. Tom went through his routine of wall passes, trying to add to his record number of touches without losing control. Then he took free kicks aiming at different parts of the 'goal' that his mind's eye could see so clearly on the wall.

It was the shot to the top-right corner that brought the practice session to a sudden end. Tom had not reckoned on the growing power in his right foot, and the shot cleared the 'bar' and the top of the wall. His special ball disappeared into the old man's garden and Tom seriously wondered if he would ever see it again.

For a long moment he stared at the wall, and then he remembered the wall round Jericho in the story he'd heard the day before. God was still the same, they had said in church. He answers prayers today! So Tom prayed. When he opened his eyes, the old man's wall was still there. No way had opened up in it for him to get his ball. Perhaps he had gone about his prayer in the wrong way. Perhaps he should try earlier in the morning with a trumpet. His friend Scott had a bugle! Tom turned towards his house.

'Tom, there's someone to see you,' called his mum from the kitchen. She directed a fair-haired boy of about Tom's age down the garden.

'His name's Kevin,' she added by way of introduction.

Tom could hardly believe his eyes. Kevin was carrying his autographed football.

'I'm staying with my uncle over there,' said Kevin nodding in the direction of the wall. 'You were lucky. The ball landed near the compost heap and not the greenhouse. Uncle says I can ask you to tea if your mother agrees. He's got a brilliant pool table.'

Tom had taken in each item of information with mounting enthusiasm. 'Yes, please,' he said. 'You don't play football as well, by any chance?'

'I'm our school goalie,' answered Kevin.

'Well, I'm certainly glad this wall didn't fall down,' Tom blurted out, and then, when he saw Kevin's puzzled expression, he said quickly, 'I'll explain later. Let's go and ask Mum about tea.'

Tom understood that God was still answering prayer. He had his ball back, it looked like he had a new friend who could try to save his shots, and maybe Kevin's uncle would be a little less lonely as well.

Helping children get to grips with the story

★ What do you think Tom imagined would happen to his neighbour's wall when he prayed?
★ How was Tom's prayer answered in actual fact?

Ways for children to express the story

★ Find out how the Israelites overcame Jericho. The story is reported in chapter 6 of Joshua, the sixth book in the Old Testament part of the Bible.
★ Make a diagram of a practice wall for improving games skills.

Helping children to own the story

★ What are some of the most powerful things you can think of?
★ What kind of power was at work in the Bible story Tom heard in church?
★ What kind of power is at work in Tom's modern-day story?

Ways for children to live out the story

★ What powers can you think of that do not rely on physical force and muscle strength?
★ Talk in a group about prayer. Perhaps these might be ways to start you talking: 'Prayer helped me because I remember praying and…' or 'I don't find praying easy because…'

The glory is yours

A winner after all

Bible link

Athletes work hard to win a crown that cannot last, but we do it for a crown that will last for ever.
1 CORINTHIANS 9:25

Tom looks forward to sports day. He especially looks forward to the end of sports day, as that's when they have the longest race—the mini-marathon. You only go in for it if you really want to, and the course is right round the outside of the school field and round the outside of the school building itself.

There's something about long-distance running that appeals to Tom and nearly everyone else as well. Even those who choose not to run watch keenly and show their support. Parents, too, seem to turn up the volume of their support. The winners are mobbed and their achievements celebrated.

'That's the race I most want to win,' said Tom to his parents as sports day came nearer.

When the mini-marathon began, Tom knew he mustn't set off too fast—he must keep something in reserve. But he found himself in front and no one seemed to be keeping up with him. He heard his name being chanted across the field, and then he was behind the school. Just as he was emerging into the supporters' sight again, Tom was conscious of the rhythmic beat of feet behind him. Another name was being chanted with his own.

'Ellie! Ellie!'

He had a race on his hands after all. Tom kept his lead into the finishing straight, but the slight upward slope of the final 50 metres sapped his reserves of energy. His legs would not respond. Ellie had paced herself that bit better and swept ahead in the final 10 metres.

Ellie received her well-deserved congratulations; even Tom managed to say something, but inwardly he knew the bitter disappointment of defeat. Of course, he would have liked the backslapping and delight reserved for a winner.

A quarter of an hour later, Tom was on his way home, head down and still upset. He wasn't walking very fast, but even so he caught up with Mrs Garland, who lived a few doors away from the Wetherbys. Tom didn't realize his neighbour was there until he knocked into the shopping bags she was carrying over her arm. Indeed, Mrs Garland apologized to Tom.

'Why, it's Tom, isn't it? From just down my road. You're looking as weary and worn out as I feel.'

Tom emerged from his sports day world and its defeat.

'I'm sorry, Mrs Garland. I was miles away. That's a heavy load of shopping. Let me help you with it.'

Even the usually independent Mrs Garland was ready to receive help. It seemed to her that the shopping was getting heavier and heavier by the minute. Tom took over the lion's share of the bags and chatted as they made their way through the local streets.

'What was all that cheering about at the school this afternoon?' Mrs Garland wanted to know.

Tom reported the events of sports day.

'And how did you get on, Tom?'

Tom recounted the running of the mini-marathon and his eventual defeat. Mrs Garland remembered sports days of long ago and memories of her own school days. Tom found her really interesting to talk with. When they arrived at Mrs Garland's house, Tom volunteered to take the shopping inside and put it on to the kitchen table. Mrs Garland was very grateful.

'I'm about to make a speech!' she said. 'You may not quite have won your school's mini-marathon, but you've certainly come first in the shopping bags marathon. And I know which I think is more important.'

It was quite a speech for Mrs Garland to make, and Tom smiled his thanks. Not all marathons take place on a sports field, he thought to himself.

Helping children get to grips with the story

★ What are the things you should remember when you are running a longer race rather than a sprint?

★ Why does Tom enjoy chatting with Mrs Garland?

★ Can you put into your own words what Mrs Garland meant in her 'speech' at the end of the story?

Ways for children to express the story

★ Do a piece of writing or have a discussion about the subject 'Coming second'.
★ Collect some newspaper and magazine pictures that show people winning… and losing.

Helping children to own the story

★ The Olympic Games award gold, silver and bronze medals. What would it be like to finish fourth?
★ Can you remember times when you would have liked to have done better?

Ways for children to live out the story

★ If you are watching a competition, what would be good to say to the competitors afterwards?
★ Do you always need others to recognize your achievements?
★ What other things do you think God would be pleased with, besides carrying shopping for an elderly neighbour?

Now and for ever. Amen

found after all

 Bible link

Your kindness and love will always be with me each day of my life, and I will live for ever in your house, Lord.
PSALM 23:6

....

Tom can't work time out. Sometimes it zooms along like an express train rattling through a station and sometimes it dawdles by like a tortoise crossing a lawn.

When Rob and Scott both came round for a day in the holidays, time hurtled by at first. In the morning they had a three-way table tennis tournament and then a three-way magnetic darts tournament in the games room that the Wetherbys were lucky to have at the end of their garden. It was lunchtime in no time at all and Tom's mum provided, as usual, just the right kinds of food to suit the three hungry lads.

'Let's play hide-and-seek,' said Scott, when the food had all been eaten and the drinks finished. 'Tom, you be it, as it's your home and garden.' All went well. Then it was Tom and Rob's turn to hide. Tom knew that the shelf in the shed was deeper than it looked and that he could crouch quite comfortably on it, so he did.

Scott soon found Rob and they joined forces to search out Tom. Twice they came right inside the shed without spotting Tom in the shadows on the shelf. Then all was quiet again in the shed.

Tom began counting to himself to pass the time. Then he remembered Mrs Evans challenging him in maths at school about the highest possible number he could get to. He'd suggested a trillion.

'And one,' she had countered.

Later on, Emma, the maths wizard of the class, had talked about infinity and Tom still remembered the word. By now, in the shed, much time had passed slowly by. It was time for Tom to give himself up. He climbed down from the shelf and left the shed for the sunshine of the garden. His mum was in the kitchen.

'They can't find me,' announced Tom. 'I'm giving myself up.'

'But Scott and Rob have gone home,' said Mum. 'I thought they must have told you.'

Tom's face was a picture of disbelief. Everything had been going so well, but now it had all gone wrong. It was one thing not to be found in a game, but quite another to be abandoned by his friends. He left his mum in the kitchen and sat by himself in the games room.

Time crawled. Maybe it had partly been his fault for staying hidden so well and for so long. He would make contact by text.

That evening, the shock of being left by his friends clung

to Tom. He had sent a text to Scott and Rob. They had replied and had arranged to meet up again the next day. Tom glanced out of his bedroom window. He breathed in sharply. A most amazing sunset was filling the sky. The sky was not cloudless, but the sun shone through ridges of clouds.

It was as if the sky had become the sea, with the clouds making a harbour for voyaging yachts. When you made the first harbour, you would look out to another… and another… and another. Places of safety after places of safety. Places of welcome. Places of belonging. Perhaps going on into infinity!

Tom closed his mobile phone. The afternoon shock of abandonment was fading. Tom was feeling found again, found and safe.

Helping children get to grips with the story

★ When does time seem to go quickly for Tom?
★ When does time seem to go slowly for Tom?
★ Why does he feel better by the end of the story?

Ways for children to express the story

★ Can you remember a time when you felt lost or even abandoned by your friends? Talk about it.
★ Draw a picture of a natural wonder such as a sunset.

Helping children to own the story

★ What are enjoyable ways to spend time with your friends?
★ When does time seem to pass slowly for you? Are they always unhappy times?

★ Can you think of occasions when time seems to have gone by quickly, even though you've been on your own?

Ways for children to live out the story

★ It was a marvellous moment for Tom when he saw the special sunset. Have you ever had a moment like that, which has really cheered you up? Look out for them around you. When might they happen and what might cause them to happen?
★ What makes you feel really safe?

The prayer of St Francis

Lord, make me an instrument of your peace

Grandma

 Bible link

You lead me to streams of peaceful water, and you refresh my life.
PSALM 23:2b–3a

Tom Wetherby's grandma always has time for him and his sister. She's a good cook, and whenever Tom and Charlotte visit her, there are always some of their favourite cakes and biscuits in a tin. When Tom was young, he used to play lots of games with Grandma: I spy with my little eye, Round and round the garden like a teddy bear—that was his favourite —and Hunt the thimble.

Nowadays they chat together. Grandma has a lot of stories about when she was a girl. She has a big box of photographs as well. Sometimes, Tom isn't as patient as he should be.

It was just before Christmas that Tom heard the news. He woke up to it.

'Grandma's in hospital. She's been taken ill in the night.'

Tom gathered that it was something called a stroke. Grandma couldn't talk and she certainly wouldn't be able to cope with visits from breezy, bouncy, fidgety Tom. What a shock! No visits. No chats. No sausage rolls. No flapjack. Tom felt churned up inside. He was sorry now that he'd once or twice been bad-tempered at her house. His mum and dad were upset, too, distracted and irritable.

Life carried on for Tom. Every so often, there would be moments when he remembered Grandma. He felt empty and sad, especially when he was trying to get to sleep. He heard snippets of conversation.

'She's holding her own.'

'She's managing to eat.'

'They're moving her from hospital to a home.'

'But she's so miserable. Perhaps she's losing the will to live.'

'She's being obstinate,' said Tom's dad.

'She's impossible,' said his mum.

'Grandma,' thought Tom.

In the end, Tom could stand it no longer.

'I'd like to visit Grandma,' he said.

His mum and dad talked about it with each other as if Tom wasn't there. Would it be better for him to remember Grandma as she was? Wouldn't he fidget too much? In the end, they thought a visit couldn't do any harm, so they took Tom to the nursing home.

Grandma did look so tired… and miserable. She looked different without her glasses, anyway. So different, too, without her teeth. There was no greeting and not even the glimmer of a smile.

'Had a good dinner?' asked Tom's dad in a jolly voice. Grandma was stony faced.

'Many visitors?' asked his mum. Grandma shook her head miserably.

'This is hopeless,' said Tom's mum. 'Let's find the warden.'

Tom Wetherby was left alone with his grandma. He'd worked out that she didn't seem to know much about what was going on around her now. He knew that she didn't like what had been happening to her. But what was it they used to enjoy playing together?

Tom went and stood in front of his grandma. He took her hand in his and began to draw a circle on it.

'One step...' he said slowly. 'Two steps...'

He looked up into Grandma's face and there was Grandma's smile, deep and warming, just as it had always been. Tom was just about to tickle his grandma when there was a gasp of surprise behind him. His mum and dad were in the doorway.

'Well, blow me down!' said his dad.

'After all we've tried to do,' said his mum.

'I think Grandma is better at remembering things from a long time ago than things from a few minutes ago,' said Tom.

'Well, blow me down!' repeated Tom's dad. 'If you expect me to tickle my mother "under there" you've got another think coming,' he chortled.

'Wait a bit,' said Tom's mum. 'I remember you telling me that when you were little, you and your mum used to make rabbit faces at each other. Let's see if she remembers.'

It was Tom's turn to be amazed as Mr Wetherby—his own dad—made one of the best rabbit faces he'd ever seen. Grandma smiled again and made almost as good a rabbit face back.

'Well, blow me down!' said Tom.

Helping children get to grips with the story

★ What upset the Wetherby household?
★ How did Tom's mum and dad show that their peace had been spoilt?
★ What were the effects on Grandma of her stroke?
★ What things did Tom do to start restoring peace?

Ways for children to express the story

★ Make a picture with the title 'Upset'.
★ Make a list of games you played when you were much younger. Who did you play them with?
· ★ Create a piece of writing called 'Grandma'.

Helping children to own the story

★ What are the pieces of news that you have received that have most shocked you?
★ What happens to you when you are upset? What can you do about it?
★ What could you do to help someone who is upset or feeling angry inside?

Ways for children to live out the story

★ How might we help adults we know when they are worried or upset?
★ How can we be instruments of peace when arguments, fighting or squabbles break out among our friends?

Where there is hatred, let me sow love

Tom gets into a fight

 Bible link

Love your enemies and pray for anyone who ill-treats you.
MATTHEW 5:44

Tom is one of those lucky boys who seems to get on well with everybody—even girls! It's certainly not true of all the children in Tom's class. Take Jason, for example. Jason rarely plays with the same child twice and he often stands miserably on his own in a corner of the playground. He is bad-tempered most of the time, and when he loses his temper his eyes flash hatred.

It happened one dinnertime. Mrs Evans allows her class to play football as long as they sort things out among themselves and don't bother her. Jason is a good footballer, and he was dribbling through with only Scott Stevens and the goalkeeper to beat. Scott tackled and Jason, at the same moment, stumbled on a stone. Scott came away with the ball.

'Foul!' screamed Jason. He scrambled to his feet, raced after Scott and launched himself in a rugby-style tackle that brought Scott crashing to the ground. As soon as his breath came back, Scott leapt to his feet and wrestled with the angry Jason. Jason's eyes blazed hatred.

Tom realized that dinnertime football was in danger. A punch-up like this would show that they couldn't control themselves, and Mrs Evans always carried out her threats. Without a thought of danger to himself, Tom jumped between the flailing fists, separating the battling bodies.

'Don't be stupid,' Tom gasped. 'You'll ruin it for all of us.'

The fight subsided and Scott stood silent, surprised by his own involvement in such a fight. Jason stood trembling like an angry dog on a leash. His eyes were as full of hatred as ever, but now they were not directed at Scott. They were glowering at Tom.

'You wait,' spat out Jason. 'I'll get even with you, you little goody-goody.'

Tom shrugged uncomfortably. It was one thing to stop a scrap, but it was quite another to be on the brink of one yourself. The game restarted, much subdued, and without Jason. His hunched back could be seen in the distance as he stalked off towards the classroom.

Tom was not afraid on his own account. His grandfather had taught him self-defence, so he could take care of himself. He was disappointed that someone in his own class hated him so much and so obviously as Jason now did.

Over the next few days, Jason did everything he could to niggle Tom. He called him names; he told tales that were untrue; he nudged him in queues and tried to trip him up at playtime. Tom managed to keep his cool... somehow. He was determined not to be goaded.

But then came a challenge that Tom could not avoid. Jason accused Tom of breaking Katie's clay vase, which had been much admired and was displayed by Mrs Evans on the classroom shelf.

'It certainly wasn't me,' said Tom when the broken pieces were discovered.

'If you're telling the truth,' said Jason, 'come and fight it out with me by the oak tree at five o'clock this evening. If you don't show up, you're either a liar or a coward. Leave all your friends behind. We'll sort it out; just the two of us.'

'You sort him out, Tom,' called out Scott, who hadn't believed for a moment that Tom was responsible for the broken vase. 'Give him some of your grandad's medicine.'

'What's that?' asked Jason.

'His grandad has taught him boxing,' replied Scott. 'You don't stand a chance.'

When Tom left school, he took Scott to one side and whispered that he would call at Scott's house on the way to the oak tree, as he wanted his friend to do something for him.

'But you mustn't do that. You'll be asking for trouble,' said Scott when he heard what Tom had in mind.

'But you'll do it for me,' said Tom, winking at Scott.

Just before five o'clock, Tom was at the oak tree, looking quite calm, leaning against its ancient trunk with his hands behind his back. Jason approached, eyes smouldering, but much of his bounce had faded. Tom's reputation as a fighter had worked on Jason and worried him.

'You punch me first,' offered Tom.

'Well, I've been thinking about that,' said Jason slowly.

'Let's call it a draw and tell everyone we couldn't decide who won.'

'Suit yourself,' said Tom. 'I'll get back to Scott's.'

Tom walked past Jason and, as Jason's eyes followed his enemy, his mouth gaped open. Now he could see that all the time Tom's hands had been tied tightly with a skipping rope behind his back.

The hatred in Jason's eyes turned to amazement. Jason was left with a lot to think about. Meanwhile, Tom went back to Scott's house for his friend to release him from the rope.

Helping children get to grips with the story

★ What was Tom worried about when Scott and Jason started fighting?
★ Why did Jason challenge Tom to a fight?
★ What amazed Jason by the end of the story?

Ways for children to express the story

★ Create a piece of writing called 'Jason'.
★ Make a list of playtime rules.

Helping children to own the story

★ Why is it difficult for some people to like others?
★ What are some of the results of hatred?
★ What do you think of the way Tom handled the fight with Jason?
★ Were there any other ways that Tom could have dealt with the way Jason was treating him?

Ways for children to live out the story

★ In what ways can you sow love instead of hatred? Think of examples, either from real life or imagined. Will it be easy?

★ Jesus advised, 'Don't hit back at all. If someone strikes you, stand and take it… No more tit-for-tat stuff. Live generously' (Matthew 5:38, THE MESSAGE). Should we follow that advice?

Where there is injury, pardon

Grandad

If you forgive others for the wrongs they do to you, your Father in heaven will forgive you.

MATTHEW 6:14

Tom was spending Saturday morning with his grandad. As usual in the warmer weather, they were in the workshed at the bottom of the garden. Grandad was busy making a sewing-box for Grandma and Tom was making a mug tree for his mum. As they worked, they could go on quite happily in silence or burst into a flurry of conversation.

'You're not saying much,' observed Grandad. 'What's the matter?'

Tom wasn't surprised any more that his grandad seemed to know his moods and feelings so well. It happened so often.

'Bit of trouble at school,' admitted Tom. 'Some of my friends are getting on to me, calling me names, that kind of thing. They're even making fun of me spending Saturdays with you and not playing football with them. Foggy, they call me. Foggy Wetherby! Or it might be Stormy. Stormy Wetherby!'

Grandad smiled a distant smile. 'What does your mum say?'

'Oh, she says sticks and stones will hurt my bones but names should never hurt me.'

'Yet you still feel damaged and injured inside,' said Grandad.

Tom nodded. He was pleased to find someone who understood so well.

'You've guessed how I feel,' he said approvingly.

'It's not a matter of guessing; I know how you feel. It happened a lot to me when I was your age and a bit older.'

Grandad gave up working on the sewing-box. It would be a long story. Tom was all attention.

'You see, I started going to First Aid classes, learning about bandages, emergencies and parts of the body. I found it really interesting and we had a super teacher. But there weren't many boys in the class, mostly girls.

'Eddie was my best friend and he was into football and tree climbing. He kept wanting me to be with him on Tuesday evenings, but I said no. That was First Aid night. Eddie started to make fun of me. He got the other lads doing it, too.

'"Cissy's off to First Aid," they'd say. Yes, and Foggy they called me, just like you. Anything to do with the weather, I suppose. You know the kind of thing. The names caught on and they really hurt. I couldn't do anything about it. It would have spurred them on if I had shown I was hurt.'

'Why didn't you give up First Aid?' asked Tom. 'That would have stopped it.'

'That was one thing I knew I mustn't do,' replied his grandad. 'It was right for me to go to First Aid. I was learning and remembering. Even though I say it myself, I was good at it. I knew it was worth even the hurt and the name-calling.

'I'd been doing First Aid about a year when the railway accident happened—just round the corner from our house and across the field. A Bank Holiday it was. We heard the screeching, the bang, the rumble and then a horrible silence. You just knew what must have happened, and out of our houses we ran to see what could be done. I grabbed the little case that First Aiders had.

'It was a terrible sight when I got to the field. It occasionally comes back to me in a nightmare even now. There were people running and staggering in all directions—in a panic to get away from the stricken tangled monster of a train.

'A man fell at my feet, bleeding from his head and wrist. I saw immediately that it was Eddie's dad. I knew from my lessons that the deep wrist wound was the more dangerous and I tied a bandage tightly to slow down the bleeding. He calmed down as I attended to him and then he got to his feet unsteadily.

'I propped him up as best I could and we struggled towards the road. We had just reached it when Eddie came up, as white as a sheet, yelling "Dad! Dad!" They reckoned afterwards that I had probably saved his life.'

'That really put Eddie in his place,' said Tom.

'Steady on, lad,' murmured Grandad. 'We remained the best of friends after that. Eddie was still the expert tree climber but he understood that First Aid had its place.'

'But he'd been really nasty to you, calling you Cissie and

all that. You should have put him in his place and made sure he appreciated all you'd done for his dad.'

'Oh no,' said Grandad, 'that would never do. Wars break out because people keep getting their own back. Do you know, 50 years on, I still meet Eddie from time to time. It was Eddie and his wife that we went away with on holiday last year.

'One other thing came out of it. That's where my new nickname, Sunny, started. Eddie's father wrote to the local paper about his rescue from the Bank Holiday crash and the headlines on the article read, 'Sunny Wetherby, First Aid Champion!' So not all nicknames are unkind or unwelcome, are they?'

Grandad had finished his story, and winked at Tom as he turned back to Grandma's sewing-box.

'No, Grandad,' responded, Tom smiling. 'I've got a lot to learn.'

Helping children get to grips with the story

★ For what different reasons were Tom and his grandad called names?
★ Why do you think Grandad and Eddie are still good friends? What could have upset the friendship?

Ways for children to express the story

★ What clubs and after-school activities do you know about?
★ Tom learns woodwork skills from his grandad. What skills do you learn or would you like to learn from older people?
★ Create a piece of writing called 'Nicknames'.

Helping children to own the story

★ Tom agreed that he felt 'damaged and injured inside'. What do you think that means?

★ What do you think of the saying, 'Sticks and stones will hurt my bones but names should never hurt me'?

★ Have you ever been called nicknames that you haven't liked… or that you have liked?

★ What could you advise someone to do if they're feeling hurt inside?

Ways for children to live out the story

★ Tom's grandad says that wars break out because people keep getting their own back. Do you agree with him? Can you think of times when you've forgiven someone instead of getting your own back?

★ What good advice have you received for living life?

Where there is doubt, faith

The real thing

Bible link

When you ask for something, you must have faith and not doubt. Anyone who doubts is like an ocean wave tossed around in a storm.
JAMES 1:6

Tom's birthday was several months away, but he already knew what he'd like his grandparents to give him. He'd really like Grandad to make him a wooden model of their dog, Pip.

Pip was Grandma's and Grandad's lively, likable Yorkshire terrier. That was the second most important reason for visiting his grandparents—visiting Pip. Tom missed Pip when he was back home or at school. If he had a model, it would remind him: he could stroke it and imagine Pip more easily. But Grandad would need some advance warning.

'You know my birthday,' Tom said when they were next alone in Grandad's workshed.

'Yes, it's months away,' smiled Grandad.

'I wondered if you could make me a model of Pip—only you'll need time.'

Right on cue, Pip dashed through the open door. Grandad stooped to stroke his dog.

'I'll do my very best,' he said to Tom.

As time went by, Tom wondered if Grandad had remembered. Nothing was said and his grandad never seemed busy in his workshed whenever Tom was round. After a while, Tom found it difficult to remember exactly what had been said.

Tom discussed it with Charlotte, his sister.

'Grandad won't let you down,' was Charlotte's opinion.

'I'm not so sure,' said Tom. 'His hearing's not what it was, and he may be having trouble remembering.'

A few weeks before his birthday, Tom decided he must do something to set his mind at rest. He told Charlotte, 'I'm going to look inside Grandad's workshed.'

'Steady,' warned Charlotte. 'If you're found out, Grandad will think you're not trusting him. It's like breaking in.'

'I'm going to risk it,' said Tom. 'I'll be relying on you to keep Grandad playing indoors, and I'll do the rest.'

Charlotte did her part reluctantly and gave Tom the time he needed. Next time they were alone, Tom was really fed up.

'There's no sign of a model dog. Grandad has nearly finished Grandma's sewing-box, but there's not even a piece of wood that looks a likely size for Pip. Anyway, there's not enough time now for him to make it.'

'Grandad has never let us down before—not once,' protested Charlotte.

'I bet he's forgotten,' moaned Tom. 'How else can you explain it?'

Charlotte couldn't.

The weekend before his birthday, Tom's worst fears were realized. Tom's mum asked her son, 'When Grandma and Grandad ask me how to spend the money they give you for your birthday, what shall I tell them?'

'Tell them whatever you like!' shouted Tom and stormed out of the room.

'What on earth is up with your brother?' asked his mum.

'He'll get over it,' said Charlotte, shrugging her shoulders.

Friday was Tom's birthday. Grandma and Grandad came round for tea after school. They were there when Tom arrived home. There was no parcel. Grandma and Grandad wished Tom a happy birthday.

'Your present, Tom, is in the garden,' said Grandad. 'Off you go.'

Tom dawdled almost reluctantly to the back door. Everything had gone so badly wrong. He pulled the door open and there was a blur of brown, a yapping bark and a tiny bundle just like Pip launching himself at Tom. Grandma and Grandad had followed their grandson to the door.

'Grandad and I have been thinking for some time that it's about time you had a dog of your own, Tom,' said Grandma. 'And your mum and dad agreed that it would be OK. Do you think you can manage to look after your own Yorkshire terrier? He's one of Pip's grandsons, so he seemed an appropriate choice for your first dog.'

'Oh yes,' whispered Tom, amazed at the turn of events. Grandad certainly had done his best after all!

Tom picked the small dog up and went back indoors to find his sister. She was good at caring—and trusting—so she could share in helping to look after the new arrival. What a birthday it was turning out to be!

Helping children get to grips with the story

★ What promise did Grandad make to Tom? Did he keep his promise?
★ What part did Charlotte play in the story?
★ How did Tom recognize the part his sister had played?

Ways for children to express the story

★ Create a piece of writing or draw a picture about pets.

Helping children to own the story

★ Who would you most trust to make and keep a promise?
★ How did Tom and Charlotte cope differently with the doubts that came about Grandad keeping his promise? Who would you be more like?
★ Could Tom's grandparents and what they did in the story help us to understand more of what God is like?

Ways for children to live out the story

★ How might you cope with times when you feel let down?
★ Are you trustworthy? Do you always keep the promises you make? How do you build up a reputation for being trustworthy?

A good catch after all

 Bible link

Honour God by accepting each other, as Christ has accepted you.
ROMANS 15:7

Adam joined the class just after Christmas. The class realized it wouldn't be easy for a newcomer. Most of them had known each other since nursery, and friendship patterns were firmly established. Mrs Evans was good at pointing this sort of thing out, and urged them to do their best for Adam.

'Deep down, you're not a bad lot,' Mrs Evans had said with a smile.

Adam was difficult right from the start. He clearly had an inflated opinion of himself.

'I'm good at art,' he claimed in the first week.

When it came to sketching the trees that fringed the school field, Adam's trees looked like giant lollipops. Mrs Evans was teaching the class to look closely at the formation of the branches: the skeleton of the tree, as she explained it. Adam hadn't had that kind of teaching before.

Adam was given to telling tales, too.

'Tom's eating sweets,' he revealed in one maths lesson. It turned out that Tom's mum had written a letter asking permission for Tom to have a throat sweet regularly to soothe his sore throat. The next day, Adam had smuggled in ordinary sweets that were against school rules.

You could not rely on Adam to tell the truth, either. When he failed to hand in some homework, he claimed to have lost it on the way to school. Even Mrs Evans had her doubts about that.

Tom's mum was keen that Tom should be friendly.

'That Adam looks a nice lad. Would you like to invite him to come to tea?'

'Not yet,' said Tom quickly. If only she knew what Adam was really like.

After Easter, things kept going from bad to worse. Adam was giving the class a bad name. Things kept happening with no one admitting to being the cause. Paint was spilt in the art cupboard, children's belongings went missing, and even schoolwork was being spoilt. None of these things had happened before Christmas, before Adam's arrival.

The class had to be kept in for a whole playtime when Ellie's missing skipping rope was finally discovered in the wastepaper basket. There was never any proof, but the class's suspicions were on Adam.

Mrs Evans wondered what could be done. In all her years of teaching, she'd never been quite so desperate about anything.

Then came the special rounders match. Once a year the head teacher, Mr Watson, would choose his team to play Mrs

Evans' team. It was a much-anticipated occasion. Mr Watson won the toss and had first pick of the whole class.

'Adam,' he announced.

You could hear the gasp of surprise. Adam was always the last to be chosen when any teams were picked. Quickly the rest of the teams were chosen and Mrs Evans decided that her side would bat first.

'Adam's our backstop. Tom, you go first post,' declared Mr Watson.

The rest of the fielders were marshalled to their positions and the game began. Penny was an accurate bowler and Adam fielded well right from the start behind the batsman. You had to run after the third good ball, and when Mrs Evans' star hitter missed his third ball, Adam, more quickly than it takes to tell, caught the ball and threw it to Tom. Tom was so surprised that he missed it completely and the stumping chance was gone.

Tom was embarrassed.

'Bad luck, Tom,' encouraged Mr Watson. 'Good throw, Adam.'

Five minutes later, Tom did not make the same mistake again, and he stumped Bernard out from another swift throw by Adam. Then Penny caught and bowled a second member of Mrs Evans' side. Moments later, another batsman made contact with a top edge and Adam flung himself horizontally to secure a fantastic catch and end the innings.

'Three out, all out,' called Mrs Evans. 'Change over.'

As they passed each other, Mrs Evans murmured to Mr Watson, 'That was an inspired choice of yours—Adam as wicket keeper.'

'Well,' said Mr Watson, 'I saw him make a very good catch at dinnertime off a stray hit from another group of children. So I played my hunch.'

That afternoon was the making of Adam with his class. He became an early choice in teams. Gradually, too, he fitted in. He didn't have to boast so much and he received attention in good ways rather than bad.

When it came to Tom's birthday, his mum wondered if he would like to repeat last year's cricket outing. Tom was most enthusiastic.

'And I'd especially like Adam to come.'

'Are you sure?' queried Mrs Wetherby.

'Oh yes, please. He's a good sport and the best wicket keeper for miles around!'

Helping children get to grips with the story

★ What kind of things started to go wrong in classroom life?
★ What was the turning point for Adam?
★ Why do you think Adam behaved in a 'difficult' way at first?

Ways for children to express the story

★ Write a report on the rounders match in the story, or another sporting encounter.
★ Draw a picture of some kind of catch.

Helping children to own the story

★ Can you remember what it was like to be the new person in an established group? How did you feel or behave?

★ Mrs Evans was 'desperate' about what was happening to her class. Are there things that have made you feel desperate?
★ What things are you good at, that might be a surprise to your friends?

Ways for children to live out the story

★ If a new person joined a group you belong to tomorrow, in what ways could you make it easier for that person?
★ Try to spot things that others are good at and make a chance to say 'Well done'.
★ How many times would it be reasonable to give someone another chance?

Elementary, Mrs Penfold

Bible link

Make your light shine, so that others will see the good that you do and will praise your Father in heaven.
MATTHEW 5:16

Mrs Penfold lives round the corner from Tom Wetherby. Mrs Penfold is blind; she lost her sight when she was Tom's age. She loves having visitors and Tom tries to call regularly. He is so interested in all the gadgets that help her to live normally—her clock and watch, the machine that helps her write, the bell that rings in the garden when it begins to rain, and many more.

Mrs Penfold amazes Tom with her knitting and sewing of dolls' clothes. She's a good cook, too. She had made apple crumble last week from the early apples that were ready in her garden. Tom specially enjoys apples.

'This crumble is delicious,' he said when Mrs Penfold gave him a bowl full. 'Apples are my favourite.'

'How would it be if I put an apple on my doorstep for you to collect each day on your way to school? You would have something to eat at playtime,' said Mrs Penfold.

'Yes, please,' replied a delighted Tom.

So it was. They were good apples. Tom enjoyed his playtime treat, especially as it was a gift from Mrs Penfold. All went well until one Tuesday. No apple was on the doorstep—nor on Wednesday. Tom called in on Mrs Penfold after school.

'Enjoying the apples?' she asked as soon as they sat down.

'Well, they were lovely,' said Tom hesitantly.' But you haven't put one out since Monday.'

'Oh yes, I have. And I've heard you run up the path to collect it. Wait a minute,' continued Mrs Penfold, 'I suppose it could have been someone else. You leave it with me, Tom. Call in after school tomorrow and I'll tell you how far I've got.'

Amazingly, it seemed that Mrs Penfold was going to turn detective! On Thursday morning there was no apple again, and after school Tom hurried round to call in on Mrs Penfold.

'Well,' said Mrs Penfold smiling, 'we are looking for a boy who wears trainers, chews gum and needed to wash his hands before starting work at school this morning!'

'That's Rob,' gasped Tom. 'His mum says she's too poor to buy him shoes, and he's always in trouble for chewing gum. This morning we all laughed when he asked to wash his fingers—they were all stuck together.'

'That was the honey I smeared on part of the apple,' said Mrs Penfold. 'I'd like to meet this Rob.'

'He only lives about ten houses up from yours,' replied Tom. 'I'll see if he can come now to help me clear up some of your leaves.'

'Good idea,' agreed Mrs Penfold. 'Don't say anything

about the apples.'

Five minutes later, Tom and Rob were in front of Mrs Penfold and Tom had introduced his classmate.

'Now, young man,' said Mrs Penfold to Rob, 'I understand you like apples.' Tom saw Rob blush and Mrs Penfold heard Rob's sharp intake of breath.

'It's a very nasty and wrong thing to take apples that don't belong to you.' Mrs Penfold spoke sharply. Rob didn't say a word. He just mumbled that he was sorry.

'That's the end of the matter, then,' said Mrs Penfold in her usual tone. 'Perhaps you'll collect the leaves, and you might pick the rest of my apples if you've time. Are you good at climbing trees?'

Tom and Rob had a wonderful time tidying up, then climbing to reach the remaining apples. Soon Mrs Penfold's washing basket was loaded with the rest of her apple crop. Mrs Penfold was delighted when she heard what they'd managed to do.

'By the way,' she said, 'there will be two apples on my doorstep each morning, one for each of you.'

'Oh, thank you,' responded Rob. 'I'll never take anything that's not mine again. But how did you know it was me?' He was staring up into Mrs Penfold's unseeing eyes.

'I don't live in a world of total darkness, you know, young man,' chuckled Mrs Penfold. 'My hearing is wide awake and can certainly tell the difference between someone wearing trainers and someone wearing shoes. And my sense of smell is well up to scenting out chewing gum through an open letterbox.'

'Elementary, Mrs Penfold,' said Tom. 'Come on, Rob, it's

time we were going before it gets too late.'

Helping children get to grips with the story

★ How did Mrs Penfold manage to live on her own, even though she was blind?
★ How did Mrs Penfold show herself to be a good detective?

Ways for children to express the story

★ What things would you most miss if you were blind?
★ Draw a picture of a part of Mrs Penfold's garden.
★ Design a telephone or a clock for someone who is blind.

Helping children to own the story

★ What are your favourite fruits?
★ A blind person is literally 'in the dark'. In what ways may a seeing person also be 'in the dark'?
★ When we understand how to do something, we sometimes say, 'I see.' What moments can you remember when you've understood something like that?

Ways for children to live out the story

★ Look out for ways to help people who are disabled in different ways.
★ Think of something that you find hard to do, and try to see ways to get better at it.
★ Carry out a survey among people with different disabilities to find out the sort of things that are most helpful for them.

Where there is sadness, joy

The runaway

 Bible link

'Let's celebrate! I've found my lost sheep.'
LUKE 15:6b

Mr Watson had told the story in assembly about the one
sheep that was missing out of a flock of one hundred. He
tells stories well and Tom Wetherby could live every moment
of it. He was thankful when the sheep was safely reunited
with the others. He especially liked the idea of the sheep
riding home on the shepherd's shoulders.

Mrs Evans made sure that Tom's class settled to their
numeracy work quietly and quickly. Part of it was counting
up, in 25s, to one hundred and then to a thousand. Caitlin
managed it easily and Tom wasn't far behind.

Joseph, however, rarely said anything in maths lessons.
Joseph disliked maths because he was no good at it, so Tom
was surprised to see his hand go up. But Joseph only wanted
to go to the toilet.

'Be as quick as you can,' said Mrs Evans as usual.

As the number work was interesting, no one noticed how much time was passing. Only Mrs Evans became anxious that Joseph had still not returned. She wrote a note on a piece of paper and asked Caitlin to take it to Mr Watson.

'I'll come back with you straightaway,' said Mr Watson to Caitlin when he read what was on the paper. On the way, Mr Watson looked in the boys' toilets. No Joseph. He looked carefully all the way to the classroom. No Joseph.

'Does anyone know where Joseph might be?' asked Mr Watson in as calm a voice as he could manage. Except that Joseph had gone to the toilet 15 minutes earlier, no one had any idea. Mr Watson whispered something to Mrs Evans and urged the children back to their work.

'Joseph will be back with you soon,' he assured them. Mr Watson guessed that Joseph must have run off for some reason, and began a search of the school grounds. No Joseph.

Back in the classroom, Tom had an idea.

'Yes, Tom?' asked Mrs Evans when she saw his hand up.

'Shall I go to see if Joseph's coat is hanging on his peg?'

'That's a good idea,' said Mrs Evans. 'Then go and report what you find to Mr Watson.'

Tom hurried off. One or two of his friends wished they'd had that brainwave themselves.

Joseph's coat was still on the right peg. Everything was in order in the cloakroom. As Tom made his way back through the dining area, he heard a sneeze. It came from behind the tall pile of mats that belonged to the judo club.

'Joseph!' said Tom in amazement when he went to investigate. Joseph had squeezed himself between the mats and the wall. 'What on earth are you doing, Joseph? Mr Watson is searching for you everywhere.'

Joseph was near to tears.

'I just couldn't cope with maths today. I'm no good at it and it upsets me at the best of times. But now my hamster's gone missing overnight. No sign of it anywhere.'

Tom sat with Joseph behind the mats. He felt so sorry for Joseph.

'We can't go on sitting here,' said Tom. 'They'll get worried about both of us. Two runaways in one morning will be a bit much.'

'You go back,' said Joseph, 'but leave me here and don't tell them where I am.'

'But we both need to put some maths in our brains and then find that hamster. Running away is not going to help.'

'I haven't run away,' pointed out Joseph.

'It's as good as,' said Tom. 'Come on, we'll remind Mr Watson about the lost sheep that was found.' Joseph managed a pale smile and nodded.

As Tom emerged from behind the mats, an astonished Mr Watson was hurrying across the dining area to phone Joseph's parents about their missing son.

'Behold the lost sheep!' announced Tom with some drama. Mr Watson's mouth gaped open as Joseph stumbled out from behind the mats, his eyes pleading in the direction of his head teacher.

Mr Watson was in no mood to carry Joseph back to his classroom on his shoulders, but he did listen as Joseph, assisted by Tom, poured out the story. Mr Watson knew there would be some sorting out to be done, but the most important thing was to restore Joseph to his class.

Relief swept through the class. Mrs Evans smiled.

'I was just thinking we had two missing students.'

After playtime it was literacy, but first another visit from Mr Watson. He explained how Joseph had been feeling about maths and his hamster. Joseph now realized that it was no good running away from problems.

'They have to be faced,' said Mr Watson. 'And I've just let Joseph's mum know what's been happening. She tells me the hamster has been found safe and sound, making a nest in their newspaper recycling bin. So today is very much the day for lost creatures being found! Before you start literacy, we'll help Joseph and each other to count up in 25s. Ready: 0, 25, 50, 75, 100, 125…'

Helping children get to grips with the story

★ What combination of things was making Joseph sad?
★ What reasons stopped Tom sitting behind the judo mats with Joseph for too long?
★ What did Tom remind Mr Watson about, which had happened earlier in the day?

Ways for children to express the story

★ The story Mr Watson told in assembly can be found in Luke 15:3-6. Draw a cartoon version of that story.
★ Write a story called 'The lost is found'.

Helping children to own the story

★ Remember times when joy has eventually returned after sadness.
★ What things would you like to be better at? What steps can you take to improve your performance?
★ Perhaps a box could be set up so that children can send a note to their parents or teacher about things they don't understand or are worried about.

Ways for children to live out the story

★ How can you help others to overcome their difficulties, rather like Tom helped Joseph?
★ When Jesus told the story of the lost sheep, it ended with a joyful party. How does that help us in the way we look at life?

O grant that I may not so much seek to be
consoled as to console

No fishing

 Bible link

Treat others as you want them to treat you.
MATTHEW 7:12a

Tom is the second-best chess player at school. Sometimes he
can even beat Philip, the school's number one. In their latest
match against a local school, Tom, playing at Board 2, made
a useful start but, in a rare moment of carelessness, gave
away his queen. His opponent made him pay the penalty.

Tom was the only one of twelve players from his school to
lose, and did he feel sorry for himself! All his teammates
were too excited and pleased with their own performances to
notice—except for Scott. Scott's chess wasn't good enough
for him to make the team, but he always stayed on after
school to help set up the boards and then clear them away.

'Bad luck,' said Scott, trying to cheer Tom up. 'You were
playing so well at the beginning.'

'What on earth do you know about it?' snapped Tom.
'You're not even in the team.'

The friends made their way home in silence. At the parting of their ways, Scott said hesitantly, 'Could you help me with my chess, Tom? I'm not doing anything tomorrow morning.'

'Don't be silly. Your chess playing is light years way from mine,' boasted Tom. 'Anyway, it's the Saturday I go fishing with Grandad.'

'You're so lucky with your grandad,' said Scott and set off down the road.

Tom carried on feeling sorry for himself. He dreaded Monday's assembly. The result of the chess match would be given out and everyone would want to know the name of the one loser.

It was still hanging over him like a cloud when he woke up on Saturday morning, and when the telephone rang, he felt in his bones that more bad news was in store. Tom's dad took the call, then sought out Tom.

'I'm afraid Grandad is unable to go fishing today. He's twisted his ankle.'

'Oh no,' fumed Tom. 'That's all I need. Surely he could make an effort. It's only twisted, not broken.'

'Now steady on, Tom,' said his father. 'That was Grandma phoning. Grandad can't even hobble to the phone. You go and do some tidying up in that bedroom of yours.'

Tom dragged his feet upstairs. Life was going from bad to worse. Fishing was one of his favourite occupations and tidying up certainly one of his least favourite. He moved books from one pile to another and papers from one cardboard box to another. Clothes were thrown in a heap behind the door.

When he'd finished, he decided to try to cheer himself up

by using his bed as a trampoline—a practice frowned upon by his mum and dad.

Tom's spirits revived a little with each bounce and roll, until he made a misjudgment and fell awkwardly between mattress and headboard. A searing pain wracked his leg from the ankle to behind the shin. He gasped out loud. Tears came unbidden to his eyes. He stooped to massage the painful limb. It was over as quickly as it had come.

Gingerly, he allowed his weight back on the foot. Yes, all was well. But what pain might Grandad be suffering! For the first time that morning, he felt sorry for someone other than himself. He found paper and felt-tip pens. He would draw a picture to cheer his grandad up.

Tom can be quite an artist when he puts his mind to it. 'That's something else you've got from Grandad,' his parents sometimes say.

It was a good, careful picture of a boy sitting with his grandad, fishing. There wasn't any doubt who they were meant to be. He'd take it round to Grandad that afternoon. How lucky he was to have a grandad like his. Someone had told him that only recently.

Scott! Tom suddenly felt very guilty. Perhaps Scott would be free to come round after all.

A phone call soon established that Scott would be coming at once. Tom hurried to set out his chessboard. It would be good if Scott improved enough to make the team. One of the first things that Tom would teach him would be the danger of carelessly losing your own queen. Tom smiled as he awaited his friend's arrival.

Helping children get to grips with the story

★ What made Tom so cross?
★ In what ways was Tom unfriendly towards his friend Scott?
★ What brought Tom to his senses?
★ How did Tom put things right? (To console is to give comfort to someone who's upset.)

Ways for children to express the story

★ Draw the picture that Tom drew for his grandad.
★ Make up a story called 'The consolation prize'. (A consolation prize is a prize for someone who misses out on winning, but especially deserves to win.)

Helping children to own the story

★ How can you cope with losing? Is it important to be a good loser?
★ Do you know people, younger or older, who are upset? How might you be able to help them?

Ways for children to live out the story

★ Can you remember times when, like Tom, you've felt too sorry for yourself? Instead of that, in what ways can you help others?
★ What things are you good at, that you can share with others?

To be understood as to understand

Scott's dad

Bible link

Ask, and you will receive. Search, and you will find. Knock, and the door will be opened for you.
MATTHEW 7:7

....

Tom has known Scott Stevens for many years. They started playschool on the very same day and they're still together in junior school. When it comes to birthday parties, Tom's at the top of Scott's list and Scott is at the top of Tom's. They enjoy each other's company so much that they take it in turns to go to tea at each other's homes once a week. At Tom's they usually play with his table football; Scott has a table tennis table that just fits in his extended kitchen.

Recently, though, things have changed. Scott has been less talkative, almost secretive, and very moody. He was upset about a goal he let in at table football. There's no table tennis these days as it's never convenient for Tom to go to Scott's.

'You can't come; my dad's off work,' said Scott one week. Last week he said, 'Sorry, we're in too much of a muddle. You can't come.'

Tom couldn't understand it. Mr Stevens had always been so welcoming, especially if you admired his books lining the walls of the lounge—and anyone who lives in a family gets used to muddles! Scott was also getting into trouble at school. Even Tom could tell he wasn't bothering. His work was untidy, slapdash and any-old-how.

'It's so sad, because he can work very well,' said Mrs Evans in the staff room.

When Tom tried to reason with Scott, his friend only turned on his heel and stormed off. Tom felt like chasing after him and really giving him a piece of his mind. How dare Scott treat his friend like this?

Four weeks had gone by, with Scott coming in his bad moods to Tom's house, but there were no invitations for return visits. Surely Scott should be made to understand how Tom was feeling? Tom had had enough of Scott's moodiness. After tea one day, he determined to go round and sort things out.

Tom's knock on the door was answered by the barking of Scott's dog, Jumbo, but then nothing happened for a long while. Tom was just turning away when the door opened and Mr Stevens stood in the doorway.

'Who is it, please?'

'Me, Mr Stevens. Tom.'

'Oh, Tom,' said Mr Stevens, sounding relieved. 'Scott has gone out late-night shopping with his mother. I used to go, but this wretched eyesight won't let me go any more.'

'What's the matter with your eyesight?' said Tom in a low voice, already fearing the truth.

'Hasn't Scott told you? I'm going blind and there's nothing anyone can do about it.'

'Scott's said nothing, but now I understand,' answered Tom.

'You understand what?' asked Mr Stevens.

'Oh, never mind,' said Tom. 'I'll be getting along home now.'

Mr Stevens's failing eyesight explained everything. How terrible to be waiting for blindness. How terrible for Scott to watch it happening to his dad. Tom did, indeed, begin to understand all that had been happening to his friend.

Tom decided on his course of action. On his way home, he visited his friend, Mrs Penfold, a blind woman who he went to see every week. He told her about Scott's dad and then wrote down a list of things that Mrs Penfold felt might be useful. She always seemed to manage so well that you often forgot she couldn't see. Her advice would be invaluable.

The next morning, Tom made sure he was at school early to tell his classmates all about Scott and his dad. He even told Mrs Evans. She was very grateful.

'I'd wondered what on earth was happening to Scott. Now I understand.'

Scott and Tom found themselves on their own at playtime.

'You know about my dad, don't you? He told me about your visit last night. The worst thing for him,' added Scott, 'is not being able to read books. He can't cope with that.'

Tom consulted the list he had compiled with Mrs Penfold.

'I wonder if this would help,' he said. 'There's something called "Talking Books". You can send away for CDs or tapes on which people good at reading have recorded the books for you. You can even download books from your computer on to an MP3 player.'

'That would be marvellous,' said Scott. 'It's Dad's birthday next month. I'll get Mum to write away to get some of those books sent. It will help him so much.'

Scott smiled at Tom just as he used to smile.

'Now you know,' he grinned, 'there's nothing to stop you coming round for tea tomorrow. We can have a table tennis championship again.'

'Great,' replied Tom. 'Yes, please.'

It was just like old times again.

Helping children get to grips with the story

★ Why did Tom get cross with Scott at the start of the story?
★ What changed Tom's mood?
★ How did Tom help Scott in the end?

Ways for children to express the story

★ Make a list of good things for friends to do when they meet up with each other.

Helping children to own the story

★ What reasons might there be if someone suddenly stops doing their best?
★ What sort of things might become more difficult for people as they get older?

Ways for children to live out the story

★ In what ways can you increase your understanding of people?

★ Think of someone you know who has had big changes in their life recently. How could you help them?
★ Sometimes things are too private or embarrassing to share with a group of people, but it could be good to share them with one good, trustworthy friend.

To be loved as to love

Crash!

 Bible link

Love others as much as you love yourself.
MATTHEW 22:39b

There was a time in his life when Tom had been at daggers drawn with his grandma. Partly, it was because he hit it off so well with Grandad, partly because his grandma had tried to smother him as a baby, demanding kisses and cuddles, and partly because their interests were so different. Anyway, it had made a kind of wall between them—a wall of Tom's building.

Grandma had done all she could to make friends with her grandson. She had cooked his favourite food and asked about interesting things, but Tom kept on hurting her. He got to the stage when he almost couldn't help doing it.

Grandma has a great interest in indoor plants. Her lounge is full of them, and she looks after them with love and care. Some of them flower from time to time and some have leaves that are beautiful enough without needing flowers.

Tom is fascinated by the cacti. The strange shapes of those plants fire his imagination and some of them remind him of creatures from outer space.

One day, when Tom went to Grandad's and Grandma's, they left him watching television in the lounge while they busied themselves getting tea ready. Tom was quite content as they were showing some recordings of great football goals that had been scored that season. When a goal was shown by the favourite striker of his favourite team, Tom leapt from his chair, punching the air and shouting, 'Goal!'

The shout strangled in his throat as his fist not only punched the air, but also the shelf above him in the alcove— the shelf that held grandma's favourite plant of the moment, a flowering azalea. The plant wobbled, then toppled and crashed to the carpet. Soil, stones, petals and leaves spilled out of the pot that, fortunately, remained unbroken.

Tom gasped with horror and acted in the same breath. He swept the soil back into the flowerpot and stuffed the plant on top. All the rest went into the wastepaper basket under a large envelope. He was none too soon.

'Teatime, Tom.'

Tom went into the dining room for his egg, sausage and baked beans. He had much more ordinary teas at home, but this time he ate Grandma's tea mechanically, his enjoyment spoilt by the recent memory of the crashing plant and his cover-up operation.

If only he could own up, Grandma would be able to put it right. Grandad often mentioned her 'green fingers'. 'The Florence Nightingale of the flower world,' he called her on occasions.

Tom went on eating silently, miserably. The words would not come. Even when it was time to go home, they still would not come.

'Here's something for you, Tom,' said Grandma as he left. She handed him a carrier bag weighed down at the bottom. 'Open it when you get home.'

Grandad drove him home, and when he was indoors, Tom opened Grandma's carrier bag. Inside was the most interesting cactus from her collection. There was also a note written on the label. 'I've noticed how much this cactus interests you, so I'm giving it into your care. Grandma.'

Tom's eyes watered.

'What a grandma,' he thought.

He sought out his dad.

'May I phone Grandma, please?'

'Certainly,' replied Dad, a little surprised.

Grandad came to the phone and immediately called Grandma, who almost flew to the receiver.

'Thank you, Grandma, for my cactus.'

'Oh, you shouldn't have bothered to phone about that,' said Grandma, delighted that he had.

'There's something else, too,' blurted out Tom, at last allowing the words to come. His confession poured out about the crashed plant.

'I'm sorry, especially as you're so nice,' ended Tom.

'That's all right, Tom. We heard the crash when we were getting tea. The azalea's all safe and sound.'

'You knew, and you still gave me that tea and the cactus plant?' said Tom.

'Of course!' said Grandma simply.

'Oh, thank you, Grandma. You're cool, and I really will look after the cactus. Goodbye.'

Grandma was glad that Tom put the phone down without making her speak any more. A lump had suddenly developed in her throat and tears needed brushing away from her cheeks. They were tears, not now of disappointment and sadness, but tears of joy that her grandson belonged to her again. It was almost, she pondered, as if a wall that had been between them was crumbling down. After all, Tom had said she was cool!

Helping children get to grips with the story

★ Why didn't Tom and his grandma get on too well together at the start of the story?
★ Why did Tom eat one of his favourite meals miserably?
★ Why did Tom ask to phone his grandma?

Ways for children to express the story

★ Make a list of three or four treats you have been given, like Tom's favourite tea and the interesting cactus.
★ Draw a picture of the falling plant.

Helping children to own the story

★ In what ways did Grandma go on loving Tom, even when he wasn't showing her much love?
★ Is the idea of a wall being between people helpful? Can you think of any examples?

Ways for children to live out the story

★ Can you think of a kind of a wall between you and anyone else? How might it be removed?

For it is in giving that we receive

Reverend Tom Wetherby

 Bible link

If you give to others, you will be given a full amount in return. It will be packed down, shaken together, and spilling over into your lap.

LUKE 6:38a

....

Tom was going to attend the induction—whatever that was! He'd never been to one before, and grown-ups hadn't bothered to explain to him what it was.

Tom did know there were going to be a lot of refreshments. A lot of church people were going to be involved as well. The Reverend Moody was going to be the main one. He was their new minister and the induction was especially for him. Apparently, it was quite a relief to have a new minister.

'It's about time,' said Tom's dad.

'Perhaps I won't have to do the flowers so often,' said his mum.

'I might stop visiting Mrs Bradman,' went on his dad. 'I'm so busy these days.'

Tom's mum and dad tried to keep an eye on Mrs

Bradman, who lived a few houses from them on their side of the road. She was so old, she was getting towards a century of years.

'I expect Reverend Moody will put her on his list for regular visits,' said Mum.

Tom wondered what he could give up. Boys' Brigade, perhaps? Maybe he would do less Bible reading. After all, Reverend Moody must do enough for two or three people.

It was good fun at the induction. Everyone came. There was a tingle in the air. The service was interesting, and even Tom knew that the singing was special. Reverend Moody officially became their minister. Then it was time for the refreshments. Sausage rolls! Cakes! So many different kinds of crisps! Tom was happy to be there a long time—he was one of the last to leave.

When they arrived home, Tom's mum remembered Mrs Bradman's magazine.

'I've forgotten to pop it in to Mrs B,' she said. 'Be a good boy, Tom, and take it round to her.'

Tom took the magazine and set off. It wasn't far. Mrs Bradman, as she so often did, was looking out of her window. She tapped on the window and beckoned Tom to wait.

'How kind of you. Please come in for a minute and tell me all about the service.'

It was nice indoors and Mrs Bradman was full of interesting chatter. In the end, she said, 'I mustn't keep you too long, but I did cook a batch of flapjack this afternoon.'

'I could always phone home to let them know I'm staying a bit,' said quick-thinking Tom.

'What a sensible boy you are,' replied Mrs Bradman. 'You are really ministering to me.'

Tom had heard a lot about ministering at the induction.

'Hello, Dad,' said Tom over the phone, 'I won't be long. I'm ministering to Mrs Bradman.'

'You're doing what?' demanded Tom's dad, amazed at what Tom was saying. 'Oh, all right. Be home by seven.'

Mrs Bradman brought in the sticky flapjack. It was delicious. She went on talking about such interesting things—playing conkers, finding fossils in her garden and the collection of coins she had. In a flash, the clock was striking a quarter to seven.

'Your visit has been a real ministry to me,' said Mrs Bradman. 'I haven't enjoyed myself so much in a long time.'

'It's been fun for me, too,' said Tom. 'I thought only people like Reverend Moody had a ministry.'

'You're just as good at it as he is,' went on Mrs Bradman. 'Let's make you the Reverend Tom Wetherby.'

Mrs Bradman took a piece of paper and folded it over several times. Then she fixed it with a paper-clip round Tom's neck.

'This is your collar,' she said with a smile.

Of course, when he got home Tom had to explain. It was all great fun.

His mum said, 'I'll carry on with the flowers. It's part of my ministry.'

His dad had something to say as well. 'Now Reverend Tom has taken over Mrs Bradman, I'd better find someone else to visit.'

'Bless you, my parents,' said Tom in his best minister's voice.

Helping children get to grips with the story

★ From the story, what do you think an induction service is in a church?
★ Why did Tom's parents think it was about time for a new minister?
★ What did Tom 'give' to Mrs Bradman? What did Tom 'receive' from Mrs Bradman?

Ways for children to express the story

★ Make a list of special services that a church might have.
★ Draw a picture of Tom wearing the special collar that Mrs Bradman made for him.
★ Find out about 'special collars'. Why do some ministers wear them?

Helping children to own the story

★ What other things might Tom do to help the ministry of the church?
★ What other things might Mr and Mrs Wetherby do to help the ministry of the church?
★ Think of something you have done that has ended up giving you a lot of pleasure.

Ways for children to live out the story

★ Think of ways you can help (minister to) others. Ask an adult if you could try some new ways to help.
★ Tom went to 'do a favour' for someone else, but also ended up benefiting himself. Think of times when this has happened to you.

It is in pardoning that we are pardoned

Double trouble

 Bible link

Don't condemn others, and God won't condemn you.
MATTHEW 7:1

Tom's mum and dad had been ashamed of the state of their garage for some time.

'It's a right old glory hole,' was the verdict of Tom's mum. There was no longer any room for the car. Toys and tools jostled for space with pipes and paint, sawdust and seeds with car oil and the remains of carnations.

Last week, Tom's dad decided to do something about it, and set a day aside for 'Operation Clear-Up'. He would take the junk to the dump by carloads. He even planned to carpet half the concrete floor to make a play area for Charlotte and Tom when bad weather stopped them from using the garden.

When he joined the rest of the family for lunch, Dad's broad smile proclaimed a job going well.

'There's nothing like a fresh start,' he beamed.

Tom shared his father's feelings. He, too, had been clearing up. The object of his attention was Lego, and he had collected every piece he could into a grocery box. He'd found it all over the place—down the side of chairs, in with his train set, under his bed and even by the side of the cornflakes in the larder.

In the end, he was very surprised at the amount of Lego he had, so he decided to undertake a major airport construction to show it all off. His dad admired it.

'I've just got two more planes and the passenger reception to go,' said Tom. 'Then I'll be able to chalk the runway markings on the base to finish it.' The base was all set up on their small lounge table. As the base overlapped the table a little, Charlotte was calling the underneath of the airport her pony stable extension.

It took Tom until teatime to finish his model. He really was pleased. It looked so real, and every piece of Lego he owned had been used. He taxied the aircraft along the runways and lifted them up into the sky.

'Last carload for the dump,' reported Dad. 'The garage is all tidy. What a relief!' He admired the now completed airport—and Charlotte's extension.

'Would you like to see the garage?' Charlotte was too busy with her ponies, but Tom followed his dad through the kitchen. Tom was truly amazed at the transformation his dad had worked. It was so tidy and orderly. The newly carpeted play space looked exciting. When Dad said, 'Why don't you stay here while I go to the dump?' Tom nodded enthusiastically.

In actual fact, the play area was only good fun for a little while. Tom was too old for the rocking horse and too big for the plastic slide. The climbing frame, stored by the shelves on the wall, looked more interesting. Probably it wasn't secure enough to climb, but Tom was big now and would manage.

Up he climbed, towards the shelves where his dad had sorted and arranged his paints and other containers. Up he went, wobbling a little at first, but when he was as high as the shelves Tom wobbled a lot! He grabbed the shelves, but they weren't fixed yet either.

Down came shelves, paint pots, climbing frame and Tom, landing in a heap on the carpet that fortunately broke his fall. Paints of many colours tipped together on the carpet.

Tom, unhurt, was more shaken to see the chaos he had caused in Dad's new-look garage. The blue carpet had a messy rainbow strewn across it! The more Tom used rags and water from the watering can to try to clear it up, the messier it all became. He would be for it!

Despairing, he gave up, put his slippers on in the kitchen and slowly, sadly walked back into the lounge. He sat on a newspaper on the floor and dreaded his dad's return. Even his airport failed to lift his spirits. Charlotte was organizing her ponies.

'Who'd like some of Princess's birthday cake?' she was asking in her poshest voice. It could only have been a few minutes before Tom heard Dad's car turn into the drive. He half hoped that Dad would use the front door and delay discovery, but no! It was the garage door that Tom heard sliding open. Then the back door slammed sharply. Dad was through the kitchen and into the lounge.

'Tom!'

At the same moment, Charlotte became aware of her dad's return and jumped out from under the table. Her head missed the table, but not the hardboard base of Tom's model airport. It shot up and Lego pieces flew everywhere. A day's work collapsed before their eyes.

Tom's hand, grubby and paint-stained, covered his mouth. Charlotte screamed her loudest scream in horror. Her head was all right, but she feared the wrath of her brother.

'I'm sorry!' she shrieked.

Tom gulped back his anger and did something he rarely does. He put his arms, messy though they were, round his sister.

'Never mind,' he managed. 'You couldn't help it.'

Over her shoulder, Tom looked imploringly at his dad, framed statue-like in the doorway. Dad's anger stayed for only a second or two longer and then he had his arms round both his children.

'Never mind,' he said to his son. 'I guess you couldn't help it either!'

Helping children get to grips with the story

★ Why were Mr Wetherby and Tom working so hard?
★ Why might Tom and his dad have been so angry towards the end of the story?
★ How, in fact, did the story end for both father and son?
★ Which is worse: the child who deliberately takes one bite out of the apple pie in the fridge, or the child who accidentally knocks the whole pie on the floor?

Ways for children to express the story

★ Create a piece of writing called 'The hard work of clearing up'.
★ Draw a picture of either the tidy garage or the Lego airport.

Helping children to own the story

★ Remember times when you have made a mess of things and needed to be forgiven.
★ Where do punishments fit in?
★ What about times when others have upset you? What has happened next?

Ways for children to live out the story

★ Next time someone upsets you or hurts you, what are you going to do about it?

It is in dying that we are born to eternal life

The butterfly

 Bible link

God loved the people of this world so much that he gave his only Son, so that everyone who has faith in him will have eternal life and never really die.

JOHN 3:16

Tom's class was having an especially good school year. It was their last year before secondary school. They had always worked well together, but somehow Mrs Evans was bringing the best out of them.

As a teacher, Mrs Evans is an all-rounder. 'Jack of all trades, master of none,' she comments ruefully in the staff room. She follows up the children's interests so well. In the autumn, when the stinging nettles on the wasteland by their school were besieged by caterpillars, they soon had a few of the furry creatures inside their classroom, housed in a vivarium with growing stinging nettles providing their food.

Elizabeth had been keenest on this particular project. She spent minutes at a time gazing at the caterpillars. She was the first to see one stiffen in a cocoon and become like a tiny wooden puppet.

It was towards Christmas that Elizabeth became ill, not with chicken pox or anything like that, but really ill. Mrs Evans discussed Elizabeth's illness with the class. They always found her discussions helpful.

'Elizabeth has gone into hospital for a serious operation,' Mrs Evans told them.

It was a brain tumour that had to be removed. Everyone was pleased when the doctors declared the operation a success and Elizabeth started to get better.

Towards Easter, Elizabeth came back to school just for the mornings.

'We'll have to take special care of her,' Mrs Evans pointed out. 'And make sure the vivarium is clean and tidy!'

Elizabeth had changed a lot. Her hair had fallen out and she did need to rest in the afternoons to regain her strength. She was still, however, the bubbly personality she had always been.

'You won't get rid of me that easily,' she said with a grin.

Elizabeth retained her interest in the caterpillars, too. All was still and motionless inside the vivarium. It all looked most unpromising. Mrs Evans encouraged Elizabeth to find out as much as she could. She read books and even contacted a local naturalist.

Every so often she would report the results of her research to the class. Elizabeth kept them enthralled with her discoveries. She drew detailed pictures of the butterflies that would eventually emerge. She was confident that it would all happen before their eyes in the summer term.

The class were shocked that Elizabeth was not in class after Easter, not even for mornings.

'I'm afraid the doctors have found more problems in Elizabeth's body,' reported Mrs Evans. 'She's staying in a London hospital and everyone's doing the very best they can for her.'

Tom felt, with his class, a sense of helplessness. It all seemed so unfair. Mrs Evans asked Tom to move the vivarium on to the shelf by the window so that it would receive light and warmth.

It was at half term that Elizabeth died—in the hospital in London. All the children had heard about it before they returned to school on the Monday. Mrs Evans mentioned it briefly and then set her class to their day's work.

At the end of the afternoon, Mrs Evans was beginning a new book with them that she would read as a serial. In a quiet moment, there was a low crackling sound from the windowsill. Even Mrs Evans' attention was drawn to it.

There was a fluttering in the vivarium. Flimsy wings stretched, collapsed and stretched again. Next moment, the butterfly fluttered against the window above the vivarium and rose to find the opening at the top. Outside, the butterfly soared swiftly out of sight.

Mrs Evans had stopped reading. She was as enthralled as the class. The words she spoke came easily to her.

'How Elizabeth would have loved that sight. Perhaps she can see it. If a caterpillar is transformed into a butterfly, who knows what might happen to us when we pass through death?'

Tom sighed. He could hope and smile again. It was time to go home, and on his way he searched the blue sky. He was looking for a butterfly.

Helping children get to grips with the story

★ What were Elizabeth's special interests?
★ How did Mrs Evans encourage those interests?
★ Why does the story end with Tom searching the sky for a butterfly?

Ways for children to express the story

★ Draw sketches of the life cycle of a butterfly.
★ Find a picture of a butterfly and make your own picture of it.

Helping children to own the story

★ Can you think of lessons we can learn from the animal kingdom that help us in the ways we live?
★ Is this a happy story or a sad story?

Ways for children to live out the story

★ We're not very old before we hear about death—either of people or animals. How could this story help us to cope with that?
★ How have we felt when a person or a pet we've loved has died? What helped us cope? Share happy memories of the person or pet.

Index of Bible links

Old Testament Bible links

New Testament Bible links

Resourcing **Collective Worship and Assemblies, RE, Festivals, Drama** and **Art** in primary schools

- Barnabas RE Days—exploring Christianity creatively
- INSET
- Books and resources: order Brian Sears' previous book, *Through the Year with Timothy Bear*, online.
- www.barnabasinschools.org.uk

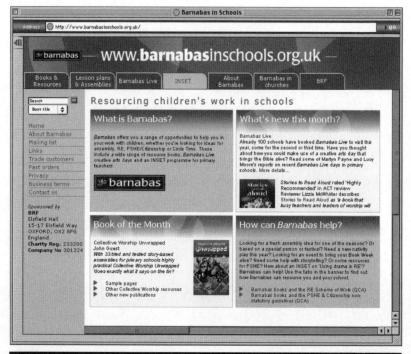